The Sp

Book 1	Sprocket and the Great Northern Forest
Book 2	Sprocket and the Great Museum Scam
Book 3	Sprocket and the Poison Portal
Book 4	Sprocket and the Heart of the North
Book 5	Sprocket and the Pax Dracus
Book 6	Sprocket and the Time Vortex

All these titles are available from Amazon.co.uk and in many other countries in both E-book for Kindle and as paperback books.

Christmas at Pudding Founders Lane is a short story available as an E-Book only.

All stories are complete and can be read as standalone books so that you can start with whichever title takes your fancy.

Sprocket and the Dragon Empress

The Sprocket Sagas

Book 7

Chapter 1	A Return is Planned	5
Chapter 2	Questions and Answers	9
Chapter 3	Plans for Domination	22
Chapter 4	Research in Depth	27
Chapter 5	Palace of an Empress	38
Chapter 6	A Visit is Agreed	47
Chapter 7	An Imperial Summons	54
Chapter 8	The Fire is Lit	74
Chapter 9	Meeting the Imperials	81
Chapter 10	Let Slip the Drones of War	96
Chapter 11	Many Words No Link	101
Chapter 12	The Blaze Spreads	114
Chapter 13	The Traveller Returns	124
Chapter 14	Invasion	137

Chapter 15	News Leaks	142
Chapter 16	Are Dragons Real?	161
Chapter 17	Beware Angry Mothers	169
Chapter 18	Progress on Some Fronts	183
Chapter 19	Flags are Raised	190
Chapter 20	Bird Watch	204
Chapter 21	The Gloves Come Off	216
Chapter 22	Resistance Begins	224
Chapter 23	Cracks Appear	233
Chapter 24	Rescue	241
Chapter 25	The Clean Up	248
Chapter 26	All Neat and Tidy	255

Chapter 1   A Return is Planned.

The small glowing dot on the radar screen was approaching rapidly from just above the range of mountains that surrounded the remote desert plateau.

"I think its time we went outside to watch the demonstration." the white-coated executive opened the door of the control centre and Quin Lee Mi stepped out into the stifling heat and trained the large binoculars on the horizon panning them across to catch any sign of movement. The dragon burst from the cloud base and dropped like a stone towards the target area that was covered with wrecked vehicles and groups of shop window dummies.

"It's very quiet." She said turning to the executive.

"That's because it is travelling faster than the speed of sound. The sonic boom will follow it in a few seconds," he explained. It flashed towards them barely twenty feet above the ground then bat-like wings shot out and it swooped up shedding most of its forward momentum. As it reached the zenith the drive flame cut just as the sonic boom arrived and the ground shook with the thunderclap. The wings folded back and it swooped across the target, a jet of scintillating gas and liquid shooting from its nose. As it levelled out a blue-white flash ignited the vapour cloud which engulfed the area in ravening fire. When the smoke and flying ash cleared very little remained of the wrecked trucks and cars and there was no sign of the dummy people. There was also no sign of the dragon either.

"Satisfactory, Most satisfying." Qin Lee Mi clapped her small gloved hands and beamed at the executive. "My wish is that the machine would be more dragon-like to be recognised as the fabled beast. When it is deployed I want the world to know that dragons have returned." The executive bowed and muttered that her wishes would be met as she stalked away to the waiting helicopter.

Qin Lee Mi sat in her vast office turning her huge, black leather, swivel chair from side to side as she scanned the panoramic view through the floor to ceiling windows which formed half of the wall of the circular room. The view would have caused anyone with a fear of heights to cling to the ornate, carved wood frame which surrounded the sliding doors of the entrance to the lift which was the only access to this nerve centre of the huge Quin-T-Sential communications, cosmetics and health food empire. Lee frowned as her gaze passed over the crowds thronging the streets far below. This should all be under her control. Her family had been rulers of China and many of the surrounding lands had paid tribute to their might and the strength of their armies. Tribal chiefs had grovelled at the base of the steps leading to the Imperial Throne and lives had hung by a thread at the whim of her ancestor's' word. Legend had it that her forefathers had ridden the skies on the backs of dragons and rained fire and death on their enemies. Now, despite her great wealth and the multi-billion turnover of her business empire, she was forced to negotiate with petty politicians, and the current leadership of her ancestral home country was threatening to impose taxes on her products to allow her entry to the massive Chinese market. Her frown darkened and the slender gnarled fingers of her left hand drummed on the polished wood of her chair arm. She would crush these upstart peasants. When the legends rose from the mists of time and once again the head of the Qin dynasty could pour fire and terror upon those who opposed her they would once again beg for mercy and the sparing of their lives.

Chapter 2   Questions and Answers

Ava had been learning about Chinese New Year at school and had been fascinated by the dragon dancers and the drummers who accompanied them. She wanted to find out more about the dragons and if they were real and if any lived in Dragon World. Most of the dragons she knew could fly but the ones portrayed in the dragon dances had no wings and seemed more like a cross between a snake and a lion. Needing answers to a pile of questions she made her way to the Pit Head and took the lift down to the lowest level of the mine workings and the striped rock wall which contained the portal through to Dragon World. Stepping from the lift she turned right and marched straight towards the massive slab of orange and ochre rock. As she neared the solid stone her steps didn't falter and as her foot met the slab, both the stone and her leg seemed to shimmer and merge. With her next stride, she became like a picture on the rock then faded into it. Ava felt nothing of this as to her eyes she moved into a short cave then out onto a rock path, high on the cliff overlooking the swathe of pinkish, red grass of the meeting ground. As usual, a huge red dragon stood before a carved wooden lectern, a quill pen in one claw-tipped hand, and a stack of scrolls spread before him.

"Hi Llewellyn," she called as she scampered down the dusty slope of the path and on to the velvety grass. The massive beast smiled, something which would make most people scream, as a dragon's smile has far too many teeth in it for comfort, bent and scooped Ava up as she ran to him. Though no words were spoken they instantly began mind to mind communication.

"Hello, small smiley person. What brings you here today?"

"I want to know all about Chinese Dragons. Do they really exist? Are there any here on Dragon World? Have they got wings and can they fly? And most of all can I meet some?"

"Slow down, please. One question at a time. This is a vast area of knowledge, and simple answers will confuse as much as enlighten."

"But we are doing Chinese New Year at school and I need to know all about these dragons so I can write about them and draw really good pictures in my folder."

"You are asking for a lifetime of learning in seconds and though I can show you some, I am not an expert on all matters Dragon and we will need to consult the library and talk to the actual dragons to give you a true picture of their history. This cannot be done in five minutes."

Ava looked somewhat downcast.

"Do not be sad and please, no sulking. We can find answers to all your questions and arrange to meet some of the Chinese Dragons, but you must be patient and learn things in the right order so that the answers make sense and lead to full understanding. First, Chinese dragons do exist and there are many on this world, but they live far beyond the Great Forest on the other side of the Purple Ocean, more than two days flying to reach them. They are a secretive race due to a long history of persecution and almost being wiped out before finding their way to this safe world. We must first contact them and ask permission to visit and they will only meet with the agreed representative of the Grand Council so it may take a few days. Let's see a smile? We can make a start in the Library. Follow me."

Placing Ava back on the grass he turned and walked towards one of the vast slabs of polished basalt rock which jutted out from the cliff face which towered above the red grass plane. Ava followed him needing to run and skip to keep up with the dragon's steady, ground-eating strides. They arrived at an area of the black, polished rock which had a border of intricately carved vines and flowers. There was no obvious door, only a finely traced outline of a dragon's clawed hand. Llewellyn placed his left hand over the outline and a fiery line sprang up from the ground to their left, leapt upward, across then down on the right. For some moments nothing happened as the fire line faded, then with the sound of a long, breathy sigh, the huge rock slab slid inward by a meter then hinged to the right as soft dim light was revealed. They stepped inside and the light gradually brightened as they walked further into what was now revealed to be the biggest cavern Ava had ever seen. Even the sound of her heart beating seemed to echo in her ears, yet it was so silent that she could have heard the footfall of a spider creeping across its web. But there were no spider webs here.

Not a speck of dust anywhere, Just row upon row of racks like a honeycomb, each segment containing a neatly rolled scroll, its end cap inscribed with a curly golden script which Ava couldn't make head or tail of.

Llewellyn went to a large stone table, the top of which was made up of small circular tiles, each with a different curly character engraved into its surface. He scanned them then reached out and touched one of his cruelly sharp talons delicately onto a tile. Instantly the tiles began to shuffle and reform into a small area containing some twenty tiles outlined in a border of blank, black tiles. The dragon stared at these for a moment, obviously committing them to memory then strode off between the rows and blocks of honeycomb towers which rose higher than Ava's eyes could focus. She followed him tiptoeing in the silence of the vast cavern. She was so fascinated by the patterns of red, white, and grey veins running through the black marble flooring of the cavern which seemed to pulse and made it seem alive that she almost tripped over the dragon's tail when he stopped in front of one of the towers. He reached out with his left hand to a cylindrical column at one side of the tower and slid a talon into a circular hole in its top. To Ava's surprise, the floor on which they stood began to rise smoothly till Llewellyn removed his claw then it stopped. He scanned the rows of hexagonal compartments removing several scrolls some of which he gave to Ava to hold. Having selected about two dozen he placed a talon into the hole of a similar column on the right and the floor descended.

They made their way to another area where they laid the collection of scrolls out on the polished surface another stone table. To Ava's amazement, the scrolls remained flat and didn't curl back again.

"Look." came the dragon's thought.

Ava looked, but couldn't make any sense of the strange blocks of flowing curled script.

"Join your mind to mine and see through my eyes." came his thought, so she relaxed and flowed into the dragon's mind. Suddenly the letters made sense. Pictures formed in her mind and the answers scrolled across her thoughts. She had to concentrate hard as the information flowed so quickly but, it seemed to stick and not fade as so often happened when she was trying to remember spellings for tests. It wasn't in the form of just words or pictures. Nor was it like watching a film or the television but more like a vivid dream or a favourite memory. What she was seeing, hearing and understanding had the same reality as if she was living every minute. Now Ava could understand what her cousins Victoria and Kate had tried to explain when they were told things by the Foresters or the big dragon, Golden Friend with whom Victoria spent many hours in conversation. Facts flooded in to fill all the areas which her questions had created and caused other questions to arise to be filled by more information. It all made sense because the enquires were triggered by the need to fully understand and built her picture of the Imperial Chinese Dragons as if she was being raised ever higher so she could see further.

The torrent of ideas gradually slowed and stopped and as it did she became aware that what she now needed more than anything was sleep so that her mind could catalogue and index everything she had been shown. Her head slowly sank to the surface of the table and she was immediately sound asleep. Llewellyn scooped up the slumbering child and carried her back through the cliff face door returning to his lectern on the grass of the meeting place where her father, in answer to a dragon thought, was waiting to take her home to bed.

It was still quite early on Sunday morning when the light over the wardrobe in Kate's room started to flash indicating that her cousin wanted to come through the portal connecting their houses. Kate was amused that since her older sister had moved to her own bedroom on the top floor she had to ask permission to use the portal. Kate never refused, but it was satisfying to have the option of veto on the use of the portal. Being the middle child of three she rarely had total control over what happened and this small power pleased her.

"Come on through," she called as she rolled out of bed and pulled on her dressing gown.

Ava burst out of the wardrobe obviously bubbling with excitement and instantly began to pour out her experiences of the previous day while her cousin was still rubbing the sleep from her eyes and looking for her slippers.

"Hold on till I give Victoria a call or you'll have to go through it all over again," mumbled Kate who was half under her bed fishing for her left slipper.

"Go call up the stairs, but don't bother with Gil, he takes forever to wake up and all you'll get is moaning from him for at least another hour. I'll follow you up when I've found my slippers."

Ava flew through the door and bounded up the stairs to wake the eldest cousin. When the three girls were gathered in Victoria's room Ava began to pour out the story of her experiences in The Library on Dragon World. Neither of the older girls had ever been in The Library having garnered their knowledge of dragons and dragon lore from Golden Friend, in Victoria's case, and the slow-moving tree-like Foresters who tended the woodlands which Kate spent most of her free time with. Ava described the secret door in the cliff and the seemingly endless rows of scroll towers with their lifting floors to give access to the multitude of hexagonal compartments. Her cousins fired questions at her to get a better understanding of this vast store of written information and when their younger relation began to describe how she had looked through Llewellyn's eyes to read and understand what she was seeing both the other girls confirmed that they had used the same method to gain understanding from the golden dragon and the tree keepers.

So engrossed were they in the new information Ava was recounting to them they were surprised when Jill, Victoria, and Kate's mother called up the stairs to ask if they were ever coming down for breakfast. There were three places set and, as Gil had already left with his Dad to go to Rugby practice, and Jill had spoken to Ava's mother to let her know where her daughter was. The three girls sat down and began to gobble up toast and cereals like a plague of locusts.

Between mouthfuls, the trio decided it would be worth going to visit the dragons to see what progress had been made in contacting the secretive Imperial dragons. Kate and Victoria scurried off to their rooms to get dressed for the outing while Ava proceeded to tell her aunt about her school project in great detail. By the time her daughters came back fully dressed she had been supplied with far more information than she would probably ever need about the traditions of Chinese New Year. When the three girls went off to the portal under one of the willow trees by the pond on the village green, Jill heaved a sigh of relief for the silence and the fact that the dragons would be providing lunch for the three ravenous appetites heading their way.

Chapter 3 Plans for Domination

Lee Mi wrote the meticulous Chinese characters of her signature at the bottom of each of a stack of documents which would set in train the transfer of the headquarters of her vast corporation from the United States of America to an insignificant, rocky spur in a warren of islands in the South China Sea. Her lawyers had spent months establishing ownership of this outcrop and had poured millions of dollars in bribes into countless secret bank accounts in a web of tax havens to acquire the thick pile of documents necessary to prove beyond contest in any court in any country on Earth that it belonged to Quin-T-Sential Corporation. Her secretary exchanged that folder for a second one which contained numerous engineering contracts that would transform the barren islet into an unassailable entrance to a vast underground/ocean office and research laboratory for the development of countless new projects she was now putting into action.

All this had been triggered by the breakdown of talks between America, China, and several other Asian countries regarding trade terms. This had resulted in the announcement of yet more tariffs and taxes on the trade, import, and export of goods and services between the various nations. Previously it had been enough to offer financial inducements to one or more officials on either side of a trade deal to turn a blind eye to the movement of her companies' products. Now America and China had leaders who seemed determined to wreck each other's international trade so that the rest of the world would see which one was the top nation. Lee Mi had lost patience with the petty posturing of the two men and any respect she had for those who wielded political power on either side of the arguments had long evaporated. She scanned and signed the last document of the second folder and passed it to the man waiting at her elbow.

"Issue the instructions immediately and make sure that all involved understand the consequences of failure to carry them out in the required time frame." The secretary bowed and walked quickly and silently to the lift doors in their carved wooden frame. As the doors closed noiselessly behind him, Lee Mi smiled a tight, humourless smile. Her Secretary was totally loyal to her. No-one would ever get him to tell her secrets as he was a mute whose tongue had been cut out in prison as punishment for challenging the treatment of his sick mother. She had found him on the verge of death from hunger and the diseases which were rife in the obscure labour camp which she had been shown to encourage her to line the pockets of the corrupt government official in return for a free slave workforce when she was just starting in business. She had purchased him body and soul, had him nursed back to health, and given him a top-class education. Later she had arranged for the official to be the victim of a particularly gruesome accident. The skeletal prisoner had grown to be an intelligent, resourceful, and devoted employee on whom she could rely entirely. Her gaze moved to the panoramic view down the long traffic-jammed canyon between the high rise office blocks and the ever-present layer of fumes and pollution which hung over the crowded metropolis. She shivered as she contemplated leaving this distorted mockery that its inhabitants thought of as the Free World. Who would want freedom if its price was to have the air choked from your lungs? When she ruled justice would be exact, swift, and final. The world would be better for it.

Returning to her desk she opened a compartment in the ornate underframe to reveal a line of compartments containing several ancient scrolls. Extracting one, she unfurled it and began to read. The ancient pictograms detailed the ritual her ancestors had used to summon their war dragons. For many years now she had collected anything that could be discovered regarding the Qin dynasty and its links to dragons. Her corporation had secretly funded research programs in numerous universities around the world, funded their explorations and archaeological expeditions to uncover her ancestral past. At last, things were falling into place and an increasingly detailed picture was forming of the reality of dragons and how Qin Warlords had used them in combat. If she could tie down the details of the summoning ritual she could dispense with mere technology and bring the world to heel with the terrors of legend.

Chapter 4 Research in Depth

Llewellyn could hear them coming before the chattering trio even came out of the portal cave. A vast, ever-expanding cloud of questions and speculation proceeded the girls as they ran down the path to the red grass lawn on which he waited by his lectern and scroll table. The thought which overwhelmed all others was the desire to visit The Library.

"Hush, hush, please. You are asking for so many different answers it is making my head spin." The large, red dragon clasped his talons over his pointed ears though it was not the sound of voices which was causing him distress, but the maelstrom of three streams of endless questions.

"SILENCE!" His mental demand halted their babble as if someone had slammed a door. "Now, first things first. Yes, you can explore The Library, But!" and he held up his hand with its deadly display of claws to stop the inevitable onset of more questions. "You will need a claw each and you must learn to read our language and script."

Llewellyn looked down at the three despondent faces and tried not to laugh at the thoughts of having to spend days if not years learning to read in a totally new language that didn't even use the same alphabet or symbols. Kate, ever the practical one was trying to work out how many months it would take to grow a useable talon.

"Follow me," he said and set off across the red velvety grass towards a row of caves sheltered under the trees which fringed the meeting place. He paused at the third cave along and tapped on the open door.

"Come right in Llewellyn." came a thought from the dim interior "And bring the students with you."

The girls arrived at a trot having fallen behind the large dragon.

"In you go and follow the instructions that Grey Scale gives you. He is the expert on our language and script having studied the contents of the Library for the last five hundred years. He is also in charge of teaching young dragons how to read and write, so if he can get those young scamps to concentrate you three should be no problem. I will be back soon to take you to the Library." Ignoring the barrage of questions bubbling from the three minds the red dragon backed out of the cave.

"Just do as you're told and everything will become clear." was his parting thought as he headed back to his scrolls and lectern.

Grey Scale was tall, thin and so old that he seemed almost a shadow of a dragon. He ushered the girls to rows of couches and told them to lay back and relax. When all three were comfortable he began to hum a quiet and complex melody, the notes rising and falling, sometimes quick trills then slow harmonies which faded in volume to almost silence. As he sang he swayed from side to side, his clawed hands weaving complicated patterns in the dim light if the cave. The girls were transfixed by the song and the dragon's waving hands which seemed to leave sparkling after images in the air. Slowly, softly their eyelids began to droop and their breathing slowed and became deeper. Before they were aware of what was happening, all three were asleep.

Skeins of glowing, curling script flowed and twined across their minds joining and parting with moving images of dragons. Dragons of all shapes, sizes, and colours, were swooping and soaring through the skies, bursting from cloud banks, rolling and twisting through the sparkling air. Others walked or ran over hills and valleys while still more delved or slumbered in deep dark caverns and all the time the curling characters of the dragon's language wove its intricate pattern through and around the consciousness of the sleeping children. Without any apparent effort on their part, the letters began to make sense, to connect pictures and actions. Reasons for what the dragons were doing became clear and the aeons of dragon history unfolded in their understanding. Gradually the dream began to fade and suddenly they were awake. It seemed as if no time had passed but equally, they were ravenously hungry and when they walked blinking into the sunlight it was obvious that the sun was high at its noontime zenith.

Llewellyn was waiting for them and escorted the trio to a table under a spreading blue tree where a selection of fruit, nuts, slices of bread, buns, and dips had been laid out read to feed their hunger. It was Kate who asked the first question after some minutes of silent eating. Swallowing a mouthful of breadstick and cheese dip she looked up at Llewellyn and asked: "Now we know your language how do we get into the library and operate the lifts and scroll tables, we haven't got long pointed claws, just short stubby fingers?"

Ever practical, in the back of her mind Kate thought how good it was to be able to communicate mind to mind so that you could talk perfectly clearly even when your mouth was full of delicious food.

The red dragon opened one of the many pouches on the tool belt he always wore and produced a roll of soft cloth. Laying it on the table he carefully unfolded the material to reveal six hollowed out talons that looked exactly like his own.

"How did you get those? I thought that when dragons die there are never any remains and everything turns to dust." thought Victoria.

"You are perfectly correct, but these are not pieces of dragon they are made from dinosaur bone stained and polished to look like the real thing. Place one on the index finger of each hand and you will be able to operate all the instruments in the Library. All of the machines need to be able to detect a life force in the operator and your fingers will slide far enough into the talons for you to be recognised while the claws are long enough to operate the controls. All you need now is for me to open the door and you can start your research." rows of razor-sharp fangs flashed in the sunlight as Llewellyn grinned widely but the girls were used to dragon smiles and laughed and jumped up and down with excitement. They rapidly finished up the remaining food and followed the animated mascot of Wales to the polished slab of black basalt. Llewellyn laid his hand on the faint tracing on the rock and as before the line of fire sprang up and outlined the entrance to the Library. The massive slab moved inward then hinged away to give access for the three girls to enter the vast cavern.

Victoria and Kate stood awestruck at the vista of row upon row of towering honeycombed pillars with their scrawled contents.

"How are we ever going to find what we want in this lot?" murmured Kate.

"Follow me," said Ava grinning as she strode off towards the index table with its mass of sliding symbol tiles. With her cousins watching she demonstrated how to form a question for the table to solve then stepped back as the tiles moved and shuffled to give the location of the information she was seeking. Ava explained the coordinates and how they related to the rows and towers of the scroll storage system, then jotting down the numbers and letters on a pad she had taken from a pocket on the side of the table she led the way to the scroll study table with its special surface which stopped any scroll laid on it from rolling back up while it was being looked at. Victoria and Kate went back to the index to input their inquiries while Ava followed the details on her pad to the stipulated tower then inserted her talon into the column on the left of the honeycomb face. She counted the levels as the floor slab she was standing on gradually rose and as she neared her destination pulled the talon out of the hole on the column's top. The slab halted and she studied the symbols beneath each hexagonal segment until she found the ones she needed. She consulted the second row of symbols which gave the locations of the other scrolls she needed. It took a bit of ascending and descending before she had all the information the index table had listed but at least they had all been in the same tower and if she had been as tall as Llewellyn they would have all been in reach. Not being more than four metres tall she had needed to move the floor slab several times. Ava took off her rucksack and put half the scrolls into it then hitched it back on her shoulder. She tucked another four under her left arm but left the remaining five on the floor as she needed the talon on her right hand to bring the slab back to ground level. As the slab settled seamlessly into the Library floor she scooped up the remaining scrolls and headed back to the reading table. Arriving, she found that her cousins had already filled most of the available space with their scrolls and she looked around for more space. Off to her right two symbols glowed in the dark striated floor. Going to them she recognised that they were the dragon script of + and -. Ava tapped the + sign with her right foot but nothing happened. Thinking for a moment she realised that these would be like the other tiles and would need to be touched with a talon. She bent forward and tapped the + with one of her talons and a soft purring came from behind her. Turning she was in time to see a second scroll table rise from the floor. Extracting the first scroll from its case and spreading it on the table she began to read. Occasionally she came across a word she didn't understand and would tap it with a talon then tap the tile with the dragon script equivalent of ? at the edge of the table and an explanation would illuminate in the table's surface. She made notes on her pad as she went along and the more she read the easier it was to recognise the script and the words it formed. From time to time, one of her cousins would come and ask her about something they had found or she would go to them with a question. Several times the girls returned to the towers to replace scrolls they had finished with or to find new ones when their research lead down a different track. The combination of the script and the moving pictures the tables generated from the scrolls was endlessly fascinating and time flew by without them realising. All were astonished when the red dragon returned to tell them that it was time for them to return home and could hardly believe they had been studying for so long. They hurried up the path, said their goodbyes, and walked through their portal towards home and tea.

Chapter 5 Palace of an Empress

It was time to move to her new headquarters and Lee Mi was impatient to perform the rituals to summon real dragons. She ordered her car to meet her at the underground garage exit of the lift which connected only to her penthouse office. When the doors opened she stepped straight into her limousine the door of which slid shut behind her. As she took her seat the safety harness automatically slid around her and locked into place while a mobile workstation with touch screen and voice control rose and hinged down from the left-hand armrest. The intercom light blinked and she instructed the vehicle to take her to her private jet. Although a large, muscular man sat behind the steering wheel in the driver's seat he had no part in controlling the car. It was fully automatic and relied on satellite navigation from her own satellite network, and an encircling array of sensors built into its streamlined exterior for speed and traffic control. The man in the front was there for her protection only and to prevent being stopped by the police for using an unguided car. Next to him sat her mute, personal assistant who accompanied her wherever she went. The limousine moved off smoothly and entered a tunnel, the doors of which opened at a signal from the car and closed after it. Emerging some miles from the outskirts of the city, and joining the multilane highway to the north, the vehicle accelerated to the speed limit and swept onward into the countryside. In less than half an hour the coastline and ocean came into view and the limousine eased over to the exit lane and left the highway at a slip road marked for maintenance vehicles only. It rolled down a slope to a pair of large steel doors set into the side of a hill which opened as its approached. The car's headlights came on automatically, revealing a tunnel descending into the darkness, and the vehicle picked up speed as the metal doors slid shut behind it. Fifteen minutes later the journey ended as the car halted in a large metal hanger containing her jet transport. The limousine rolled slowly up the open rear ramp and into the aircraft. As it halted, clamps locked the wheels in place and the ramp rose to seal the fuselage. Lee Mi closed the programme she had been running on her console and it folded back into the armrest. The safety harness unlocked, slid away and the door opened. She stepped out of the car and walked along a corridor into the plush passenger compartment and took her seat, the safety harness automatically closing around her as her secretary took his place across the aisle. The guard went through to the crew compartment and shortly the plane took off.

"We will be coming in to land shortly." The pilot's voice cut through Lee Mi's thoughts.

Please make sure your seatbelt is secure as it may be a little bumpy with the crosswinds."

She looked out of the window to see lines of white-capped waves rushing to surround a jagged rock fang thrusting up from a maelstrom of spume and spray. As she watched a gaping hole opened in the rock wall. As if a biblical prophet had smitten the waters with his staff a long tongue of steelwork capped with concrete rose from the waves connecting with the gaping cavern. The view was lost as the aircraft banked to line up its approach and in a matter of moments they were taxiing to a halt inside the cave. A covered airbridge connected to the door of the plane and Lee Mi released her harness and, followed by her assistant walked up the sloping corridor to be met by the chief engineer in charge of her new headquarters.

"Everything is as you specified Mam," said the white overalled man bobbing his head with respect to this tiny woman who ruled his every action and paid his very large salary.

"Give a full update to my secretary and make sure that all details are included. I will want to inspect the summoning chamber in one hour. Make sure the acolytes are prepared and in attendance."

"Yes, Mam." The engineer handed a memory stick to Lee Mi's assistant then hurried off along a side corridor to carry out her commands.

She continued toward her office along a corridor carpeted with what appeared to be a striped fur in shades of cream and beige. Along the walls hung a variety of oriental works of art, all originals and all of immense value. These were just part of the fabulous collection that Lee Mi and her ancestors had amassed over generations. As the last surviving member of the Qin dynasty, all this was hers.

This was her palace, a place of comfort and luxury which few others would ever see. Perched on top of a fang of volcanic rock thrust up from the seabed aeons ago by a long-dead volcano it had been a barren hazard to coastal shipping till she had purchased it and lavished a fortune on converting it to an impenetrable fortress where she could be safe from the world. There were no landing places to approach by sea and the sheer smooth granite cliffs rose vertically from the vortex of battling currents which surged around the junction of rock and ocean. These liquid forces churned the surrounding sea into a maelstrom of crashing surf and murderous whirlpools which shipping kept well clear of. The summit had been first cut off flat, then carved and hollowed into an intricate series of groves and gardens surrounded by the natural rock of the island. Within this ecological paradise had been built a relatively small but sumptuous dwelling capable of providing for her every comfort. Lee Mi occupied the two floors visible above ground with services and staff accommodation taking up the first two basements. Below these were a warren of storerooms, cold stores, and fuel silos. This was a fortress with stocks of food water and energy supplies to last for years even if all links with the outside world were severed.

Entering the main living space she turned to her assistant who had followed her and was now arranging various files and documents on the highly polished, lacquered top of a curved wooden desk which with its padded leather chair sat on a section of the floor which could turn to face any part of the room.

"When you have finished with my papers, arrange with the chief to have my meal ready when I have inspected the summoning chamber, then you may retire for the evening."

The young man, Chan by name, bowed, finished arranging the files, and silently left the room through a door which, when closed formed part of the floor to ceiling bookcase covering one wall. Lee Mi sat in the large leather chair, reached forward, and pressed a series of buttons set into the underside of the desktop causing parts of the surface to slide allowing three screens and a keyboard to rise and switch on. She worked steadily for the next hour ignoring the impressive sunset visible through the panoramic window overlooking the manicured perfection of the gardens. When a soft chime sounded she closed down the desk with a wave of her hand restoring its surface to a seamless display of intricately inlaid patterns of different woods. She rose and exited the room through the same hidden door her assistant had used.

Chapter 6   A Visit is Agreed

More than a week had passed since Ava had first visited the Library on Dragon World and though she was yet to meet any of the reclusive Chinese Dragons her researches had provided more than enough materials to finish her project for school. She had taken great care with her drawings making sure that every detail was correct and that her writing about the legends of dragons in Chinese folklore matched with the facts she had found in the Library's scrolls. Carefully placing everything into her dragon folder she placed that into her school bag ready for the next day. Tomorrow was Friday and she would hand in her project, it was a shame she had still not met any of the real beasts but none of her school friends or her teacher knew about Dragon World so it would make no difference to her finished work. Still, it was a shame not to have come face to face with the real creatures. She made her way downstairs for some supper before bed. Entering the kitchen, she climbed onto one of the high stools by the breakfast bar where a plate with some of her favourite cookies and a glass of cold milk were waiting for her. No sooner had she made herself comfortable and picked up the first cookie than the flap in the kitchen door slammed open and a very excited, small Scrap dragon burst in.

"It's arranged. You can see them. We go on Saturday. It will take all weekend. They're huge and nobody's seen one in ages." The babble of overlapping thoughts that the small dragon was broadcasting was so loud they made Ava's head spin.

"Slow down Sprocket. One thought at a time. What are you on about?" Ava leaned down and scooped the small dragon up, then stroked his head to calm him. Nuzzling close to her Sprocket took a couple of deep breaths then exhaled a string of pink smoke rings.

"I've just heard from Golden Friend. He was the one who The Grand Council asked to make contact with the Imperial Chinese Dragons to ask if you could meet them. He heard from them today and they have agreed to a meeting. You will need to be at Dragon World early Saturday morning so we can leave as soon as the sun rises."

Holding Sprocket under her arm, Ava jumped down from the stool and ran to find her Mum and Dad to tell them the great news and ask permission to spend the entire weekend with the dragons. When she had explained all about the proposed visit, how long it would take, and who would be going with her she held her breath and waited for their decision. Neil and Louise looked at each other, then smiled and said yes.

Friday dragged by as Ava's excitement built and Sprocket was bouncing up and down on the doorstep when she got home. After she had completer her homework and gobbled down her tea, her Mum shooed her from the kitchen.

"You better go and pack your rucksack and make sure you pack some warm clothes, you know how cold it gets when the dragons fly high and fast. Will you need food for this trip?" asked her Mum. The small dragon shook his head and Ava confirmed that the dragons would provide all she needed in the way of food and drink.

"In that case, you'd better get upstairs to bed as you will have to be up with the lark tomorrow, and don't forget to clean your teeth." said her Dad smiling as she scampered off to her bedroom. Seconds later she was back.

"Sprocket's staying in my room tonight so I wake up at the right time tomorrow. That's ok isn't it?"

"Fine." said her mum "Now off you go to bed. Your Dad will be up in ten minutes for the bedtime read."

The thunder of footsteps receded upwards.

In the island fortress, surrounded by its maelstrom of boiling surf, most of the staff were asleep. Lee Mi was prowling back and forth in front of a large screen as she waited for reports to come in from several research projects which had nothing to do with cosmetics or health foods. This was the basis upon which she intended to resurrect the power of her ancestors and bring the Qin Dynasty back to its place as ruler of China and in time the entire world. Across the top of the screen was a row of clock faces showing the time of day at each of the secret research establishments. Each was working on a small part of the project and had no idea of the final use their work would be put too. Chan sat bowed over the keyboard of his laptop rapidly typing in and transmitting the questions to which Lee Mi wanted answers from the heads of the various teams. He was also extracting information from the surveillance videos which were downloaded from the satellite links to all the operations. Everything that happened in the laboratories and testing grounds was automatically recorded and transmitted to Lee Mi's fortress. Nothing could be hidden from the all-seeing eyes of the cameras and the ever-listening microphones. Two of the lines of research had reached a successful conclusion and all the results and documentation had been transmitted, one had been a blind alley and it was clear would lead nowhere. She turned to Chan and chopped her hand to signal for him to cut the communication channels. As the screen segments went blank he looked towards the frowning woman and waited for her instructions.

"Delta 9 and Gamma 14 are successfully concluded and we have all the data and results?"

Chan nodded silently.

"Terminate both sites and send in the sanitising squads immediately. There is to be no trace left. Sigma 4 was a dead end. Eliminate the site. Make it look like an industrial accident and leak the result to the other teams to make sure they understand the price of failure."

Chan's fingers flew over the keyboard and termination orders went out. Within the hour no one involved in the work would be left alive and nothing bigger than small gravel would exist on any of the three remote sites. No witnesses. No clues.

Chapter 7 An Imperial Summons

Ava was sound asleep when a wet forked tongue wriggled in her ear and warm, damp, breath tickled the hairs on the back of her neck interrupting the warm fuzzy dream she was enjoying. Still half in dreamland she swatted aimlessly at the intrusion but the small dragon avoided her flailing hand and continued with his wakeup efforts. Eventually, she rolled over and opened one eye.

"What?"

"It's time to get up."

"No, it can't be. It's still dark."

"Yes, but we have to be in Dragon World before sunrise and your dad is downstairs making breakfast. So move!"

With that Sprocket popped a small pink steam ball at her and giggling she rolled out of bed. Seated at the breakfast bar Ava wolfed down a large bowl of cereals and two croissants with jam while Sprocket made short work of a dish of assorted rusty nuts bolts and washers moistened with a cup of sump oil then sat back on his tail while his digestive system made an assortment of worrying pops, whistles, thumps and gurgles which in any other creature would signal serious illness, but in Scrap Dragons, were totally normal.

Louise made sure that Ava had everything she needed for a long day on Dragon World including plenty of warm clothes and a hat with flaps to cover her ears. She would be flying for a long time and despite the normally warm weather in the parts, the children normally visited this journey would take her daughter high over the range of mountains which were just a faint blur when seen from the entrance to the portal cave. When all had been checked and stowed in her rucksack, Ava kissed her mum goodbye and, followed by Sprocket, hurried off to meet her dad at the pithead lift.

"Hi Dad," she shouted to the figure waiting at the pithead lift Rubbing his hands to keep warm in the damp cold of the pre-dawn.

"Come on." he called "Those dragons will be wanting to get a start as soon as you get there. You don't want to keep them waiting."

Ava and Sprocket ran into the large steel box of the lift while her father closed the outer door then the inner lattice door and pressed the button for the lowest level of the mine workings. Nobody spoke as the lift descended as it made too much noise to allow for normal conversation. When the lift stopped and her Dad opened the two doors, girl and dragon scampered across to the huge slab of striped rock which marked the entrance to the Dragon World portal.

"Wait for me," he called collecting a large electric lantern from the rack by the lift. "It will be dark on the other side and you don't want to trip and fall before you even start."

The trio walked steadily towards the solid slab of rock and as they approached it seemed to thin and shimmer. Ava felt the carved wooden bracelet she wore on her left wrist grow warm and she stepped into the rock without any resistance to her progress. If anyone had been watching them the three figures would have appeared to fade into the surface of the slab becoming like a picture on its surface which then faded leaving no trace at all. To them, it seemed that in a single stride they moved from the mine workings into a short cave lit by glowing fungus high on the walls and then out onto a rock path which wound down the face of a steep cliff. Her Dad had been right, it was dark with the black sky winking with millions of stars and way over to the right a faint crescent of one of Dragon World's three moons was just setting. Below they could see six dragons milling about around a fire. Each held a long metal rod with a variety of fruits and vegetables skewered on it and they were toasting them over the flames. This was a dragon breakfast and each creature would consume at least a dozen for a normal day, but this would involve a long flight so a large pole of skewers had been prepared and the pile was going down fast.

Ava and Sprocket jumped the last part of the path landing on the springy red turf and ran towards the dragons. The girl radiated greetings and reply thoughts came back. The large golden dragon used one of his sharp talons to spear a choice morsel from his skewer and held it out to Ava.

"Try this, small, smiley person then help yourself to a skewer or two. We have a long day in front of us. For Sprocket, there is a bowl of metal turnings, rust, and mixed ores over there for you and help yourself to as much ash as you please."

Neil, Ava's Dad arrived and Llewellyn, the larger red dragon took him over to the pile of skewers so that he could join the feast.

The dragons ate fast paying no heed to the scalding temperatures of the food or the occasional flame or smouldering ember. Neil and Ava had to be more careful both with the heat and which of the array of spicy dips laid out on the table they could eat. Something which a dragon found pleasant could in many cases take the skin off the inside of a human's mouth but Llewellyn showed them which ones to try so all went well.

By the time the first glimmer of the new day began to lighten the horizon all was ready for takeoff. Three of the dragons had saddles fitted and would take it in turns, to carry Ava while two more wore straps with a T bar on top so that Sprocket could perch when his flames ran low but for most of the time he would fly. The formation would be a lead dragon followed by a diamond four with Sprocket in the middle of that. Ava climbed onto her saddle sliding her shoes and legs into the high boots and tightening the straps. Llewellyn handed her a hood lined with soft wool padding and a built-in visor, it also had a tube that connected to a device around the dragon's chest which collected oxygen and fed this into the hood. Ava leaned down and kissed her Dad then he helped her to put on the hood and fasten the straps. She pulled on large gauntlets which came right up to her elbows and gave one last pull on her lap strap before taking a firm grip on the hand loops on the front of the saddle.

"Are you ready?" came the dragon's thought

"Yes," she replied and the giant beast leapt into the air bringing its wings down with a clap like thunder.

They speared into the sky followed by the four other dragons and Sprocket and glancing down Ava could hardly believe how quickly they had climbed, her Dad and the other dragons already seemed no bigger than ants.

"How do I turn on the oxygen if I need it?" she asked the dragon she was riding

"You won't need to. As we get higher and the air pressure drops the device on my chest will automatically feed more air and oxygen into your mask. Your ears may pop as we rise so hold your nose and blow." His thoughts were warm and reassuring.

"Just like being in an aeroplane?"

"Exactly."

Ava settled into the comfortable high-backed saddle and checked the straps of the harness. She could see for miles in all directions. Far below, to the left was one of the many lakes of Dragon World and among the waving milk palms along the beach, she could see a group of dinosaurs collecting the milk sap from the palms which they used to make the many varieties of delicious cheese she so enjoyed. Away to the right was the Great Forest its many shades of different coloured leaves spreading away to the misty outlines of the towering' frozen peaks of the mountains where the Ice Dragons lived.

Peering over Golden Friend's shoulder to see where they were heading there were heeps of cloud piling over each other to such a height that she had to lean back and crane her neck but still could not see their tops. The dragon's powerful wings beat up and down its huge muscles driving them ever onward, though when Ava looked down the ground below seemed to pass quite slowly. Only the power of the wind of their travel, which, but for her harness would have plucked her from the saddle gave a hint of the speed of their flight. The steady whoosh and slap of the dragon's wings began to lull the girl and soon she drifted off into dreams of soaring above the land on her own wings spiralling ever upward to dodge and swoop among the stars which spangled the dark blue of the sky.

Ava was jerked back to reality by the sensation of dropping like a stone and she had to fight down the feeling of panic as the ground appeared to leap toward her. Golden Friend was diving toward a long green valley high among jagged grey peaks of a range of mountains. At the last moment, his wings snapped out, his head on its long neck came up and his powerful hind legs shot forward and down to execute a perfect landing on the short flower speckled turf of the valley floor.

"Time for lunch." came the comforting thought as the other dragons settled around them as softly as thistledown.

As usual, the spread was lavish with many of Ava's favourite dishes and plenty of new ones to try. Sprocket made a beeline for an aluminium tray full of rusty old bolts and metal turnings liberally doused in paraffin and sump oil. Thrusting his duck-like beak into the pile he began to vacuum up the oily mess with every sign of rapt enjoyment. Golden Friend pointed out the dragon specials to avoid as they would be far too spicey for humans. The local baker who produced lunches for the dragons who worked in the recycling centre in the bottom levels of the mine had once let her try a tiny amount of one of the toppings he used and it had been three days and many glasses of milk before her tongue had recovered and the dreadful taste had left her mouth.

When lunch was over and the dragons had repacked their loads the group took off again. They flew in a spiral gaining height and very soon Ava realised that she was breathing enriched air through her mask and as she looked up the sky was changing to a darker blue and she could see stars winking. When she looked down it was bright daylight and she realised that the dragons must be reaching the upper limits of Dragon World's atmosphere.

The dragons spread out into a V formation and with long sculling strokes of their vast wings began to cross the towering, ice-clad peaks of the mountain range. At one point they were joined by a trio of young Ice Dragons who flew alongside swooping and performing stunts and aerobatics which made Ava gasp and clap her hands. For a while Sprocket joined them, his tail jets weaving patterns of condensation trails across the dark freezing sky.

"Young showoffs!" came the golden dragon's thought. "But they are children and need to practice their flying skills and learn their limitations. We will be starting to descend soon so you will need to relieve the pressure on your ears. You know how to do that?"

Ava did. Her parents had shown her how to squeese her nose and blow till her ears popped and she could hear properly again. She knew she would have to do this several times as the air pressure increased the lower they flew. It was the same as when they had flown on aeroplanes when they went on holiday. These days they usually travelled by portal whenever possible. It was free, there was no hanging about in airports waiting for flights and baggage but she did miss the thrill of takeoff and landing.

The dragons flew down from the mountains sometimes weaving between the fang-like peaks and skimming low over colls and passes till at last they cleared a vast waterfall. Breaking free of the mist and spray rising from the torrent they came to a wide plain crisscrossed with streams and rivers flowing from the mountains. Away in the far distance, Ava thought she could see the glint of sun on water but she wasn't sure.

The squadron of dragons flew on and soon she began to doze as the sun sank toward the horizon.

She awoke to what appeared to be a blaze of fire and almost panicked till it became apparent that it was the reflection of the evening sun from hundreds of faceted glass domes and towers. They had reached the land of the Imperial Dragons.

"Ah you are back with us." thought Golden Friend. "When we land and you meet the first dragons remember to bow low. It is a tradition and good manners with Imperial Dragons and they are very particular about their rules and traditions. Do not speak unless you are spoken to and keep your thoughts in check. Don't smother them with a cascade of questions as you sometimes do with Llewelyn and me. You must take things very slowly. The senior dragons are centuries old and are used to being treated with great reverence by their kind and will take offence at the smallest things. So you must be very careful when you meet them."

"Are they all like that or are there different kinds of dragons like the Seekers and Artisans?" asked Ava

"There are two main kinds." thought Golden Friend. " The ones which fly and the ones that don't. The flying kind is the Imperial Dragons and they rule this region and form the administration of this area and the upper ranks of their military and society. The other kind that your world thinks of as Temple Lions are the ones represented in the lion/dragon dances at Chinese New Year. They do most of the work and make this society operate. You will meet both types but we will spend most of our time with the Temple Lions. They are more friendly and more fun." there was a grin in the big golden dragon's thought as he swooped down to land in front of the welcoming committee followed two by two by the rest of the dragon squadron.

There to meet them were two winged Imperial Dragons and four Temple Lions. The larger, older Imperial Dragon stepped forward and Golden Friend bowed low to him. Ava, who had released her harness and slid to the floor also bowed deeply keeping her thoughts as still as possible. Dipping his head slightly the lead dragon bid them welcome and the golden dragon raised his head. Ava also straightened up but kept her eyes downcast.

"I am Fi Chin, leader of the guard of the Imperial Palace. My attendant, Chen Lee will be your educator in Imperial protocol and will introduce you at official functions. The Lion guards will guide you to your quarters and see to your needs. Do not stray from their care. Breaking the Imperial Code is severely punished and ignorance of the rules is not a defence. I leave you in their care as I must attend to my duties." Without further, he turned his back on them and left the courtyard.

The younger dragon stepped forward and stamped his perfectly manicured foot. "Follow the Lions to your quarters. Do not stray. You will be summoned in due course." With that, he too turned his back and marched away.

One of the Lions stepped forward and bowed to Golden Friend. Ava looked at him closely. When it moved it used all six of its limbs to walk, but when it stopped it raised the front part of its body standing on the back four legs becoming nearly four metres tall. In bowing it lowered its head till it almost touched the floor.

"Please excuse our Imperial masters they are not intentionally rude but are so governed by their strict code of rules they become almost panicked when asked to step outside their normal routine. Nothing has changed for their kind for centuries. It is we Lions who have adapted to dealing with the outside world." He grinned showing a huge number of sharp white fangs which, if Ava had not been used to dragon smiles would have been terrifying. She grinned back at the Lion who winked at her and made her giggle.

The procession set off. One lion at the front with Ava skipping alongside him followed by seven dragons and two more lions bringing up the rear. The streets they walked along were paved with decorated bricks depicting many Chinese scenes in blue and white which Ava recognised as being similar to the pictures on one of the tea sets in the glass-fronted cabinet in number 7 Pudding Founders Lane where Brassroyd, her great uncle lived. Eventually, they came to a large grass area in front of a tall building that Ava knew was a pagoda by the many layers of scoop-shaped roofs. Surrounding each floor level were heavy railings made of tree trunks smoothed and polished. Ava wondered about this and the Lion by her side picked up on her thought.

"They are for dragons to perch on. What you are looking at is a dragon roost. These used to be common all over the old country and were where the Dragon Emperors kept their war beasts. Every brigand who could collect together a band of fighting men would build a dragon roost in the hope of obtaining a war beast to fly into battle on. Few ever did as finding and training a fighting dragon was a rare skill which few people ever survived long enough to master. many an aspiring dragon master was eaten by his beast or simply flamed out of existence by a grumpy trainee. These days our roosts stand empty because it is beneath the dignity of an Imperial Dragon to be mastered by a mere human."

Ava sat chatting to the lion while the dragons with the aid of the two other guides sorted out their accommodation. Finally, tiredness from the long journey began to overcome her mountain of questions and the lion showed her to the rooms on the ground floor of the pagoda which would have been used by the roost supervisor. She was shown to the bedroom where she slumped onto the large bed and was instantly asleep.

Chapter 8   The Fire is Lit

Qin Lee Mi sat in front of a bank of monitor screens reviewing the daily reports from her sprawling business empire. To her left at a small desk sat her mute assistant his fingers poised over a keyboard to input her instructions and reactions resulting from the information on the screens.

"Tell the stockbroker to increase our holding in Control Software and trade off our futures in Cassava Root. We have more than enough for our production needs." At her command, the assistant's fingers flew across the keys and the terse instructions were acknowledged within seconds. None of her employees or service providers would hesitate to carry out an order from Lee Mi, the consequences of slow response would be instant dismissal for individuals or the blackening of the reputation of a company. She switched to another set of screens which contained updates on the development and readiness of the dragon attack drones. She studied the production figures from the component manufacturers. Three were behind schedule and there was a growing possibility that production of the finished drones would be slowed down. Everything had to be ready for the launch of her campaign at the start of the National Party Conference when all the political and military would be away from their posts and unable to organise a rapid response. Nobody would dare to take decisive action without direct orders from their leaders and this would give her a major opportunity to spread terror and chaos across the rural areas before turning her weapons onto the cities to demonstrate the inability of the Party to protect its people.

She turned again to her assistant.

"Suppliers three, eight, and fifteen are falling behind their production targets. Issue the warnings and prepare the team to carry out replacement and termination if targets are not immediately met."

Her assistant nodded and his fingers flashed over his keyboard sending out the messages which would strike fear into three boardrooms. It would not just mean the loss of orders but the end of life if results didn't improve. Any manager or director who had thought that orders from Quin-T-Sential were a license to print money was about to see the true meaning of the small print on the contracts.

Lee Mi closed the screens and rapidly read through the pile of printed reports making notes in neat Mandarin Chinese characters on each which her assistant would translate into actions and plans in whatever language was appropriate to where the receiving company or division of her operation was based. This finished she rose from behind her ornate desk and strode to the lift to make her rounds of the security and defences of her island retreat.

The reefs and tidal flows around the upthrust fang of volcanic rock on which her base was built ensured that the sea for several miles around was a continuous maelstrom of huge waves, ripping currents, whirlpools and jagged outcrops of rock which the local mariners kept well away from. Maritime charts had the area marked a severe hazard to navigation and all the main shipping routes took a wide detour to steer well clear of the problem. This aside Lee Mi's security chief had people monitoring the sky and the sea above and below the surface twenty-four hours a day and any boat or plane straying too close to the area received loud and insistent warnings to steer away.

Lee Mi, accompanied by her security chief, walked around the numerous lookout posts receiving verbal reports of any observations made during the current shift. They then descended to the control room where the radar and sonar equipment was monitored. The only significant event was a microlite aircraft that had lost power three miles to the South. It had ditched in the ocean and had been picked up along with its pilot by the coastguard after the alarm had been raised by one of the operators using an untraceable mobile phone. Everything was as it should be and no threats had been found to the supposedly unoccupied rock.

The final part of the inspection was the summoning chamber. Deep in the rock, below sea level, a natural cave had been adapted as the site in which the ritual for summoning a dragon would be performed. Lee Mi, along with the chief engineer and the head of security stood in the observation room which was separated from the chamber by a floor to ceiling window of transparent volcanic crystal which was half a metre thick.

"As you can see Ma'am the transmitter wire is attached to a ring bolt in the arch over the Resonator Pit. The Pit goes down seventy metres into the rock and its walls are polished to a mirror finish. The termination weight is one metric ton of gold and platinum alloy. When the acolytes perform the ritual it will cause the transmitter wire to resonate at the stipulated frequency which will summon the dragon. The beast should appear on the ritual fire." Said the engineer.

"You have tested all the elements?"

"As far as is possible Ma'am, without actually performing the ritual."

"Very well. Prepare the ceremony for sunrise tomorrow. That will be all."

Lee Mi returned to her office and the constant flow of information from her business empire. She was indeed, she felt, a true Empress and the rightful heir to the dynasty of the Dragon Throne. Soon the world would know this and the political upstarts of her native land would grovel at her feet when legend became reality.

Chapter 9 Meeting the Imperials

Ava awoke as the reflection of the rising sun flashed from a polished brass statue of a dragon onto her eyelids. She sat up and stretched as the sliding door to the bedroom rattled.

"I have your breakfast. May I enter?"

"Yes please." she thought as she rolled to the edge of the large bed, stood up and straightened her pyjamas.

The door slid aside and the Temple Lion trotted in a tray of assorted dishes balanced on each of its front paws. He placed them carefully on a low table and pulled a large cushion close for Ava to sit on. As she lowered her self onto the gayly patterned cushion enticing smells wafted up from the plates and bowls spread out to tempt her appetite. A bowl with a pair of chopsticks a knife, fork, and spoon were there for her use.

She paused, her hand hovering over the small bowl.

"Where's Sprocket?"

"Ah, your small metal gobbling friend. The monkeys have taken him off to meet with the disposal crews who keep the city clean. There are a number of his kind in charge of the recycling side of the operation. He will be staying with them till the official meetings are over. The Imperial Dragons would be terribly offended at the presence of a low cast Scrap Dragon in their midst. It avoids problems and he will have much more fun and plenty to eat. Now eat your breakfast before some of it goes cold."

The Temple Lion sat back on its haunches and Ava tucked into the amazing display of food on offer.

"Use whichever utensils you feel comfortable with." said the Lion "We use our claws." and he flicked open his paw to display a quartet of long glistening talons and flashed his fang-filled grin. Ava laughed and picking up the chopsticks helped herself to small amounts from several dishes.

"You can use chopsticks?" the Lion raised his furry eyebrows in surprise.

"Yes. My parents like to go to our local Chinese restaurant and taught me how to use them. We all like Chinese food very much."

Ava bombarded the lion with questions between eating mouthfuls of unusual food and the creature did its best to answer them. By the time she had eaten her fill she had learned a lot about Temple lions and a number of the other types of dragons and animals who lived in the empire of the Imperial Dragons.

The lands which composed the empire were surrounded by the Ice Fang mountains except for where the Boiling Sea crashed incessantly against the vertical cliffs of the coastline. Because of this, the empire could only be entered by air and the dragons of the Imperial Guard patrolled the skies day and night to keep strangers out. The Grand Council of Dragons had a small Embassy in the foothills of the Ice Fang range and were allowed one messenger dragon to fly in and out each month. Their Ambassador was required to attend a meeting of the Imperial Council twice each year, but other than that was confined, along with her staff, to the Embassy and a small park surrounding it. She and they were virtually prisoners. Because of these conditions and the aloof attitude of Imperial Dragons, the post of Ambassador was not a popular appointment and any dragon serving at the embassy only did a three-year placement after which they were only too pleased to return home to the freedom of the sky and lands. The only thing which made life in the embassy compound bearable was the friendly attitude and good humour of the local Temple Lions who seemed to welcome everyone they came in contact with.

"Have you been a Temple Lion long?" asked Ava

"For two hundred and five years next birthday. Before that, I was a scarer which is much more fun as you have to keep monkeys, birds, and lizards from mucking on the temple buildings. You get to run around the grounds and climb all over the pagodas chasing away the wildlife but then I grew too big and heavy so I had to spend all day sitting on a gate post looking fierce. That's really boring. The only fun in that is growling when young monks pass to see how high they jump and how fast they run away because all the monks think we are painted stone statues. Only the Abbot of the temple knows we are real and that secret is only passed on to the new Abbot when the old one dies. The worst bit is that all the creatures we frightened when we were scarers get their own back by sitting on our heads and pooing down our backs. The first thing we do when we come off duty is to have a shower and a really good scrub." the lion shivered at the thought of what he had to tolerate in the course of his duties.

"But you are not guarding temples at the moment," said Ava

"No. Senior Temple Lions get to do visitor guarding and guiding. It's much more fun and we can laugh and play with the visitors some times." He chuckled and as he did his large nostrils glowed and puffs of purple smoke rose from them.

"My name is Ava. What's your name?"

"Keeper of the Eternal Night, but that's a bit of a mouth full so call me Ken for short." he held out a paw with claws retracted and Ava bumped fists with him and they both laughed causing more puffs of coloured smoke to spiral up to the high ceiling.

"Now I have run a bath for you as you must be squeaky clean and in your best clothes to meet with the Lord of the Imperial Host and his council. So through that door there and you will find plenty of warm towels and a dressing gown when you have finished splashing around."

Ava scampered over to the door which was four times as tall as she was and five times as wide. There was no doorknob or handle so she pushed on it and almost fell over when it swung easily away from her to reveal a huge sunken bath with steam rising from it. Quickly casting off her pyjamas she descended the steps into the warm water which came up to just above her waist. It was just the right temperature and she began to swim around exploring the swimming pool sized bath. Even at its deepest, she could still touch the bottom while keeping her head above water. She found a seat built into one side with a shelf containing a bar of scented soap and a bottle of shampoo so proceeded to wash and clean her hair. When she had washed all over including behind her ears and between her toes she swam and dived below the surface to get rid of all the suds and lather. By the side of the steps as she climbed out was a slatted, raised platform with warm air blowing from a grill underneath. On this were enough large, fluffy, white bath towels to dry all the children in her class at school. She looked around for somewhere to sit and dry her feet. There was a marble bench which she expected to be cold but when she laid her hand on its surface it was as if it had been in the sun all day and was pleasantly warm. She carefully dried between her toes and made sure her ears were free of water. There was a washbasin with a mirror at the end of the bench and she could see her toothbrush and toothpaste set out ready so she scooped up the fine silk dressing gown and put it on. It was very grand. Ankle length in front with a flowing train behind with an embroidered dragon all down one side of the front. She felt just like a princess and did a little twirl so the train floated out behind her. She cleaned her teeth carefully making sure not to splash toothpaste on her beautiful dressing gown then walked in a stately fashion back to the bedroom. She was more careful pushing the door this time but stopped in amazement. Ken had made the bed and folded her clothes from the previous day into a neat stack on a side table. What had stopped Ava in her tracks was the dress laid out ready for her on the bed. It was long, a deep emerald colour and seemed to be made of overlapping sequins so that it looked like dragon skin. The garment was laid face down to display the picture of a peacock which stretched from the high collar right down to the hem where the long tail feathers were fully spread. The whole image sparkled and seemed to be in constant movement. The Temple Lion stepped from behind one of the columns supporting the ceiling and beamed at her.

"You like it?"

"It's beautiful!" Ava exclaimed.

"Get yourself dressed and I will be back to do your hair. With that, he left the room humming a strange oriental melody to himself.

There were undergarments made from silk so fine it felt like a second skin. When she picked up the dress she expected it to be heavy but it seemed to float in her hands. The bodice was open to the waste so she stepped into the skirt then slipped her arms into the long sleeves which came to points at her knuckles. Carefully she buttoned all the row of real pearl buttons right up to her throat noticing the dragon down each side of the front. These creatures were depicted breathing fire and each flame lead to one of the buttons. Easing her feet into the silver slippers she walked over to a tall mirror on the wall between two of the long windows and turned back and forth admiring how she looked and how well it fitted. Looking up she saw Ken standing behind her grinning his fearful smile.

"It's magnificent. How did you get it made and it fits so well?"

After you meet with The Lord and his council, I will take you to meet our tailor and dressmaker. He will want to see how you look. But now we must see to your hair."

He pushed a stool in front of the mirror and Ava sat on it. To her horror, Ken flicked out his claws on both his front paws, then gently began to comb out the tangles. As he did this he breathed out softly through his nostrils which glowed while he swayed his head side to side. The warm, lavender-scented air gradually dried her hair which fell into natural ringlets which the Lion arranged into a soft flowing style which framed her face perfectly. This done he took her hand as she stood from the stool and slowly turned her this way and that watching her reflection in the mirror. Ken beamed his fang-filled smile.

"There, a proper Dragon Princess fit to grace the Council of the Imperial Host. Now we must join the others and process to the Great Hall for the meeting."

Stepping out of the tall main doors of the pagoda she saw the dragon squadron waiting for her. They had obviously taken as much care with their appearance as Ken had with hers. Their scales reflected the sunlight like multicoloured fire scintillating and flashing as they moved into formation. At the head of the line were Golden Friend and a dragon she had never met before.

"This is our Ambassador to the Host of the Imperial Dragons." Ava bowed deeply to the Ambassador.

"Take your place between us and we can get to know each other as we walk to the Great Hall. My name translates in your language as Flame Dancer." said the Ambassador.

The procession set off with Ken leading the way and the other pair of Temple Lions bringing up the rear. They followed a wide path of white tiles bordered with gold ones which wound across several parks studded with flowering trees till the gilded towers of the Imperial Palace rose before them. More Temple Lions joining the group as they approached the palace walls, till by the main gates the group of dragons was surrounded by a triple cordon of lions most of which carried golden poles topped with spears and double axe blades.

Entering the council chamber the lions peeled off to stand shoulder to shoulder around the edge of the room. The central area had eight dragon perches and one large chair. Ava and the dragons took their places and waited. Facing the dragons was a semicircle of tiered dragon perches that ascended in steps halfway tho the ornately decorated ceiling. After what seemed to Ava like hours of waiting a blare of horns announced the entrance of the Grand Council. Row upon row of the dragon perches filled with creatures all of which were covered in identical red and gold scales. They were obviously dragons as they had the powerful hind legs and wings like the dragons Ava was familiar with, but they all seemed to look the same except for the number and pattern of the black markings on their shoulders and upper arms. Their heads were different from the dragons she knew having one or more sets of horns and jutting fangs. They also seemed to have many tentacles, she couldn't think of a better word for the things which dangled from their upper and lower jaws. As the room filled Ava noticed that the higher tiers were filled with younger dragons, their scales lighter in shade, and more shiny. The lower the level of perches the older the dragons became. Their colouring was darker in both the red and the gold scales. They had more black stripes and stars on their arms and shoulders. Also, their heads were more shaggy having even more of the facial tentacles than the younger dragons. At last, to another cacophony of horns, the Lord of the Imperial Host took his place behind the huge, golden lectern carved to look like a dragon with spread wings.

Chapter 10 Let Slip the Drones of War

The central committee of the Party filed onto the platform of the Hall of the People as the masses of delegates on the conference floor stood rigidly to attention till all the committee members had taken their seats and the Chairman of the Party took his place in front of the mass of microphones and bade them sit down. The Peoples Congress was now in session. What would follow would be days of self-congratulatory speeches about the triumph of the Chinese people over the Capitalist Dogs.

Hundreds of miles from the capital and the Congress one of the people, a peasant, was leading his water buffalo along the edge of the rice paddies back to the village where he lived. Dusk was coming on and he was looking forward to his bowl of boiled rice with some scraps of vegetables and a sprinkle of spice for seasoning. Suddenly the animal stopped. Its head went up sniffing the air and its ears swivelled to some faint noise behind. The peasant also turned, searching the dull sky and landscape for what might have caused the buffalo to stop. Nothing seemed out of the ordinary in the vista of flooded paddy fields with their whisps of rice plants bent over the muddy water.

Then out of the clouds and the mists of mythology dropped the terrifying shape of a dragon. It couldn't be real. Dragons were tales to frighten naughty children. Well, this one looked real and was terrifying him. A lance of silver fluid shot from the plummeting creature. There was a bright blue flash and a deadly chrysanthemum of fire blossomed across the paddy fields. The buffalo bellowed and bolted away. The peasant screamed and fell backwards into the muddy water of the rice paddy. Flame flowed, water boiled, mud baked as hard as a brick, and the soft green shoots of the rice crop blackened to ash. All this in seconds as the bat black shape laid waste to hectare after hectare of rice crop. Then suddenly with a blinding flash and a thunderclap bang, it was gone without a trace.

Peasant and beast broke the surface and stood in dumb shock at the devastation surrounding them. A whole year of planting gone in the blink of an eye. Smoke drifted lazily across the ash coated waters and in the distance flame flickered from the scorched remains of bushes and trees. The disaster was total. The peasant shook the water from what remained of his hair and pulled off the remnant of his smock the front of which had been destroyed by the fire even as he had plunged below the water's surface. He waded over to the buffalo picked up it's leading rope and resumed his trek back to the village.

Seargent Wa of the Peoples Army was on the verge of tearing his hair out which would have been difficult as his regulation short buzz cut made it impossible to grasp more than a single hair at a time. The front office of the local guard post was jammed with hysterical peasants screaming at the top of their voices to be heard over the shouting of their fellows. What was worse was they were screaming about being attacked by dragons. Had someone dumped some drug in the local water supply? It was getting worse. A frantic crowd was forming outside the guard post as more and more frightened people poured in from all directions. He was trying to explain to the pompous fool of a lieutenant at local HQ that he needed reinforcements but the idiot was insisting that Seargent Wa filled in the appropriate forms and applied through proper channels.

One instant the crowd was fighting to get in, the next second they were screaming and running for the river across the road. Wa turned to look out the window in the back of the office and his mouth fell open. For seconds he stood not believing his eyes then screamed and dived under the sturdy counter which had until seconds ago been his only bulwark against the screaming mob. The air exploded and his heavy uniform began to char. Wa's scream was lost in the thunder of the firestorm. A hundred kilometres away the lieutenant was shouting into a dead handset. The phone at the other end of the line along with lines of poles and the wires they had supported had been vapourised along with the army checkpoint.

Chapter 11 Many Words No Link

Ava was trying her hardest to stop her eyes from closing. The only thing helping to keep her awake was that the chair she was sitting on was so big that she couldn't reach the armrests and if she tried to lean against the back she would lay out flat. Also, the seat was so far from the floor that if she fell forward she would probably break her nose on the polished stone floor. The Lord of the Imperial Host had droned on for hours and he was being followed by what seemed like an endless line of venerable old dragons all of which had hundreds of words to say about absolutely nothing. She hadn't had any chance to ask any questions and they were giving none of the details she wanted to know. She carefully removed the fan that Ken had given her from the sleeve of her dress and opened it in front of her mouth to hide a huge yawn. Golden Friend and the

Ambassador sat like stone statues on either side of her and hadn't twitched a single scale for hours. The development of the skill of sleeping with your eyes open and sitting perfectly must be part of the training to be a diplomat she decided. Just as Ava's eyelids were beginning to droop again she was snapped awake by the blare of horns and she realised all the Imperial Dragons were standing up. The dragons on each side of her held her hands and lifted her down from the huge chair and they all stood while, starting with the Lord of the Host, the Imperial Dragons filed out one after the other. Row upon row they left the vast hall till all that remained were the eight dragons, one girl, and the three Temple Lions who were their guides.

"Food. Follow me." came Ken's welcome thought.

As soon as they were outside the hall Ken picked up the pace and led them through a side gate of the park and a couple of winding allies to a small lantern decked restaurant. Over the archway of the entrance were Chinese letters picked out in gold.

"What do they say?" Ava asked Ken as she pointed to the letters.

"Wonderful Garden of Tastes and Scents." replied the Lion "Prepare to give your taste buds a treat."

Inside were numerous small tables with big revolving circles in the centre of each laden with bowls of steaming food. most of the tables had dragon stools around them but one had just one chair.

"We will sit here," said Ken helping Ava onto her chair and moving her close to the table.

They were joined by another Temple Lion.

"This is Joy of Eternal Sun, Jes for short she is my third cousin," Ken explained

Jes bowed her head to Ava then smiled a toothy smile. "I am pleased to meet you, Ava. Your dress is very beautiful."

Ava bowed in return and beamed at the compliment to her outfit.

"Enough! I am starving. Those Imperial blowhards could talk all the legs off a centipede." said Ken unsheathing his claws and delicately spearing a fried dumpling coated in dark red sauce. There followed a long and sumptuous meal with many new and tasty flavours for Ava to try. As soon as any dish was emptied it was swept away and replaced with a new full one by one of a group of apron-wearing monkeys who moved quickly and silently between the tables and the kitchen.

During the meal, Ava kept up a stream of questions about the Imperial Dragons and how this part of Dragon World operated.

According to the two Lions the Imperials had not changed in living memory, which for dragons is a very long time. There was a huge golden ledger in which had been recorded all the Imperial Rules and nothing had ever been added or removed from it. The Imperials lived by these rules and never challenged them or deviated from the life pattern they laid down. It was down to the Lions and other creatures who lived within the confines of the Ice Fang mountains and the Boiling Sea to adapt and fill in the gaps to keep things running.

"The Emperors kept many kinds of monkeys and apes as pets and in their menageries. When the Imperial dynasties fell and the dragons began to be hunted and killed they found the portals between worlds and followed the other dragons through to this sanctuary." Jes explained.

"If the Imperials hadn't been such a bunch of insufferable snobs and refused to adapt we might have lived with the other dragons but they shunned all contact with the other Nobel Dragons and tried to enslave the smaller types so the Grand Council exiled them to this private and enclosed area. They brought all their slave and servant animals with them when they were exiled and we are their descendants," said Ken filling in while Jes ate some more food.

"How do you find out what's happening in the rest of Dragon World and keep up to date?" asked Ava, her forehead furrowing with concern. "If the Imperials only let in one flight a month to the embassy and only talk to the Ambassador twice a year, News must be completely out of date before you even hear it."

"Oh, we don't rely on those old stuffed shirts," said Jes dabbing her mouth a napkin. "We made friends with some Seekers generations ago and there are dozens of portals we can use to get news and anything else we need through them. Where did you think the cheese comes from? There are no dinosaurs this side of the Ice Fang mountains." she grinned and winked at Ava

"What the Imperials don't know they don't worry about. If it is not written in the Great Book of Rules it doesn't exist as far as they are concerned. We are not going to tell them it would only cause problems and get them all wound up. this afternoon we will take you to see some of our skilled crafts creatures and you can see where things like your dress come from." laughed Ken "When you've had enough to eat we can go. Your dragon friends have things to discuss with the Ambassador and I think you have listened to enough boring words for one visit. You will be flying back tomorrow and we have presents and mementoes to find."

"Let's go then. I'm full to bursting. If I don't walk off some of this food I may split the seams on this lovely dress."

The trio stepped into the street and Ken lifted a small silver whistle to his lips and blew it. Moments later there was a pattering of large feet on the tiled road and around the corner came a three-wheeled wagon pulled by an ostrich and driven by a large Barbary Ape sitting on a saddle above the single front wheel. Ava and both Lions climbed in and she found there was just room for her to sit between her two new friends. She didn't understand the instructions which Jes gave to the driver as Ape was not a language she had mastered but the carriage moved and she soon found that the ride was very smooth. Their first stop was at the silk makers. On entering the building Ava was amazed at the level of noise and was glad that she could communicate with the lions by thought. If she had needed to shout over the din she would have lost her voice in minutes. Jes handed her some ear muffs which cut out most of the noise and they followed Ken into an adjoining room which was hot and full of clouds of steam.

"This is where the silkworm cocoons are soaked to free the thread and wash out the gum which holds them together." he pointed to lines of big copper boilers with masses of cocoons floating in them. Monkeys with sieves on sticks moved them from one vat to the next till the threads had unravelled, when they were placed onto fine mesh drying trays. these trays passed along a slowly moving belt under constantly spinning fans which blew air through the fibres. They walked to the end of the belt where a group of spider monkeys using hands, feet and tails picked up the threads and attached them to spinning wheels each monkey had four wheels to look after and seemed to have no trouble keeping up with the flow. Each set of spinners produced a different thickness of thread that was wound into hanks and hung on a chain of hooks that moved them through to the dyeing shed next door. They passed by the dyeing shed as Jes said the smell of the chemicals used made their eyes sting and went straight to the yarn store. Ava stopped in the doorway her mouth open with surprise. It was like walking into a rainbow. Every colour and shade she could imagine was on display. You didn't come in here and ask for red there were hundreds of variations of red. and the same for the other colours. Combine that with the multicoloured threads and the ones with metallic content and the range was mind-blowing. Everywhere she looked something new caught her eye. Finally came the weaving shed. Lines of looms clattered away creating a deafening din. In front of these clattering machines ambled Orang Outangs their nimble hands and feet shooting out on long arms and legs which seemed to have more than the normal number of knees and elbows. They were lightning fast changing the warp up and down and throwing the shuttles back and forth. between all the threads. They replaced empty bobbins with full ones and joined the new threads into the weave. It was mesmerizing to watch and the quality and complexity of the patterns coming off the looms were beautiful to behold. As they handed in their ear defenders and walked back into the sunshine and relative quiet Ava felt even more splendid in the dress which so much skill had been used just to complete the fabric.

"The Imperials have no idea that this sort of thing exists. They order something and just expect it to appear. Without all this skill and the trade built upon it, they wouldn't last a month before they starved to death." grumbled Ken.

"Why do you put up with them? "asked Ava.

"Things could be a lot worse. They guard the skies and we are safe behind our mountain ramparts." the two lions nodded and smiled at each other.

"One thing has been bothering me," said Ava, frowning. " You call yourselves Temple Lions and Temple Guards but Dragons have no Gods so why Temples?"

"Ah! It is just a form of words that humans understand, and you still have carved stone Lions guarding many temples and important buildings in your world. Our Temples are in fact nurseries for the eggs and young of Imperial Dragons. When a female is ready to lay an egg she will go to a Temple where a hearth has been prepared and lay her egg in the red hot coals then she flies off leaving the egg to hatch in its own good time. Imperials are not good mothers and most eggs would fail if the Temple monks didn't stoke the fire and feed the young dragon when it hatches. Temple Lions are there to protect the eggs, young and monks, but also to protect other creatures from the very bad-tempered females and young dragons who tend to incinerate anything within a one hundred meter range. So nothing worships at the temples and everything is kept away fo its own safety."

"How do the monks survive?

"By using a combination of soothing chants and heavily insulated armour. If you were to listen to a group of monks chanting you would be asleep in seconds. It is the most hypnotically boring music which has ever been composed. It would make a meeting of the Council of the Imperial Host seem like a funfair by comparison."

Ava burst out laughing and the Temple Lions joined in snorting out clouds of pastel-coloured steam and smoke.

Chapter 12 The Blaze Spreads

The Lieutenant finally realized he was shouting into a dead phone. Since the scream from the other end, there had been nothing but a crackly whistle. He threw down the handset and stormed over to the window overlooking the vehicle park. Throwing it open he bawled at a soldier lounging against the bonnet of a jeep to stand to attention then get the vehicle round to the main doors to meet him. Minutes later the jeep was bumping at high speed along the badly maintained road leading to the area checkpoint. The occupants sat in stony silence one clinging to the steering wheel the other with a death grip on the handrail under the windscreen. After half an hour of bone-shattering driving, they topped a small rise in the road and saw columns of smoke ascending from beyond a range of low hills.

"Faster man!" Screamed the lieutenant over the noise of the straining engine. The driver didn't bother to explain that they were going as fast as the jeep was capable it would become patently obvious when the poorly maintained engine exploded and pistons came up through the bonnet.

Much to the driver's surprise, they made it to the crest of the low hills where he swerved to a stop to avoid hitting the smoking wreck of an overturned truck. This wasn't what made both men gape in horror. Smoke rose from many small and large fires scattered across the landscape. The area should have contained hectares of rice paddies but they had been transformed to rectangles of cracked mud fringed by blackened ash-covered mounds. At the foot of the hill was a dead Water Buffalo on its back with what remained of its legs sticking into the air like burned matchsticks, its belly had been burst open and the charred skin was peeled back revealing the animal's ribs burned clear of flesh. The stench of burning was overpowering and the driver scrambled from his seat bent double and vomited violently onto the road. Still stunned by the vision of Hell the officer climbed out of the jeep scrabbled behind the seat and came up with a pair of field glasses which he clamped to his eyes, adjusted the focus, and scanned the devastation. After some time he located what must be the remains of the checkpoint building only because it was the tallest pile of smoking rubble on the opposite side of the road which bordered the steaming gully which had been the river. Mud and smoke-stained scarecrows were emerging from the steam and wandering aimlessly about. The driver had recovered from his sickness so they climbed back into the jeep and followed the road down to the river and the pile of smoking ruins swerving occasionally around the remains of smouldering trees and bushes.

It was the checkpoint. They could tell from the blackened remains of the drop barrier which lay in twisted ruin across half of the road. Where the office and guard post had been, were several distorted sheets of corrugated iron from the roof and piles of broken concrete blocks. Spirals of thin smoke rose from the heap which clicked and groaned as the surface cooled. As they walked around the side of the pile they heard a faint moaning from underneath. The soldier set about pulling bits of rubble and twisted roofing away while the lieutenant hurried back to the jeep to get two pairs of heavy gloves and the spade that was strapped across the back of the vehicle. They worked hard for a good fifteen minutes until they found a gap beneath several of the roofing sheets. The driver shone the beam of his torch into the hole and a pair of eyes in a soot-stained face blinked back at him. It took another half an hour with the help of some of the survivors from the river to extract Sergeant Wa, who had been saved from the fire by two metal filing cabinets falling on him. His uniform was in tatters, scorched and covered in dust and soot but apart from many scratches, cuts, and bruises he was in good shape. Some of the other survivors had various degrees of burns and many had lost all their hair and were suffering from smoke inhalation. Only a dozen or so had died most from drowning in the river but a couple of sad charred bodies were discovered. Rescue teams were called and while they waited for these to arrive the lieutenant took down a report from Sergeant Wa.

He had been trying to calm down an ever-growing crowd of hysterical peasants screaming about sheets of fire falling from the clouds and giant flying things when the shouts and screams from outside became deafening and everyone started to rush to the river and dive in. He had turned and looked through the back window to see a huge black fire breathing dragon, yes he was certain it was a dragon, diving toward the guard post burning everything in its path as it came. At that point, he had dived under the counter and the building had exploded and collapsed on him. He remembered nothing else till he had heard the sound of boots stamping about nearby.

The lieutenant studded the notes he had made from the Sargeant and some of the more coherent survivers and shook his head. He rose from the makeshift desk he had been writing at, pulled a smartphone from his pocket, and began to wander about taking photos of everything that appeared to be significant. He wanted as much evidence to back up the report he was going to have to put in to prevent his commanding officer sending him straight to the nearest mental hospital. Dragons! he thought. Who was going to believe that fairy story? He would be lucky not to be dishonourably discharged when his report went up the chain of command. A clattering broke his chain of thought as the first of the rescue helicopters rose from behind the ridge of hills and began to circle to find a landing place. Still shaking his head he walked towards the chopper as the rotors wound down and the first medical teams jumped down from the tail ramp.

Quin Lee Mi smiled a cold smile as, sitting in her office at the pinnacle of the ocean surrounded basalt rock, she watched again the recordings from the cameras on the Attack Dragon Drones. Video from her observation satellites confirmed that the drones had caused wide areas of damage and that the response from the authorities had been too little and far too late to be of any use at all. Only eight drones had been deployed in the first raids but they had caused major damage to the rice crop across a large area. Her brokers had been steadily buying up stocks of rice over the preceding months in the names of numerous shell companies and having the grain shipped to secret storage facilities. As soon as the news broke the price of rice would rocket and the value of her trades would increase many fold. None of the grain markets had seen any pattern in the acquisitions and to date, the price had been stable. That would not last much longer and the Peoples Government would be bled white trying to buy enough to feed the millions of their soon to be starving population. She rubbed her thin boney hands together then ordered her assistant to transmit the next list of targets. Within hours more crops were reduced to ash or poisoned by polluted irrigation systems and the first of a wave of attacks on power stations and communication centres had left piles of scorched rubble in their wake.

Area Commissars were in a terrified panic. Their superiors were all attending the national conference and celebrations in The Great Hall of the People and would not react well to stories of collapsing trade and infrastructure caused by supposed Mythical beasts from the skies. No pictures had emerged of the attackers and no reports had come in from the Army or Airforce of sightings or even radar tracks of the fire breathing creatures. Many mid-level civil administrators had packed up their belongings and their families and fled across borders to avoid being held responsible for the spreading chaos. The news must break soon but with any luck, they would be well away, in hiding and what money they had milked from a corrupt system safely buried in secret foreign bank accounts.

Lee Mi was well pleased with the performance of the weapons. The dragon image projectors had worked perfectly and the stealth materials and design of the drones made them totally undetectable by ground-based radar. Nothing showed up till fire rained down from the skies and by then it was too late for any air defence system to react. By the time the first pilots were running for their aircraft, the attack drones had self-destructed to a small cloud of dust and ash particles and no trace of the terrible monsters from ancient myths could be found. All the defenders could do on arrival was to take aerial photos of the devastation which had been caused. The hypocrisy of Government By the People For the People would soon collapse under its own weight of oppression and bureaucracy. Still smiling her cold smile, she left her desk and retired for a deserved rest.

Chapter 13   The Traveler Returns.

Neil was collecting his things to walk over to the pithead to take the lift down to the lowest level to pass through the portal and collect his daughter from Dragon World when the doorbell rang. He opened the door to find his policeman friend Howard standing on the doormat.

"I need to ask you a few questions about something we're looking into. It won't take long, but it's urgent," said Howard

Neil stepped aside and gestured his friend through to the kitchen putting the kettle on as Howard sat down at the breakfast bar.

"What's the problem chum?" asked Neil as he spooned coffee and sugar into two mugs and the kettle began to rumble and steam.

"What could you tell me about this bloke?" said Howard placing a head and shoulders photo of a balding man with a large moustache on the countertop between them. Neil glanced at the photo as he filled the mugs and added milk passing one to the policeman.

"Name's Herbert Oakwood. He's a dealer in rare metals, we've sold him a few small consignments of some pretty unusual alloys and he's been chasing me for some larger quantities recently. Trouble is we get our supply from recycled scrap as you know and the stuff is very expensive so you don't find big lumps of it. The dragons have to do some really careful reclamation work to even get trace elements. So although the stuff is worth three or four times its weight in gold we didn't have the sort of quantities he was looking for. I gave him a couple of other contacts who might be able to help him and bid him goodbye. Last time I saw him was about three weeks ago."

"Mmm. Well, he didn't go far. We found him dead in a car up on Black Top with a hosepipe leading from the exhaust in through the window. He looked like a suicide till the pathologist spotted that he was the wrong colour for carbon monoxide poisoning, they usually go bright red from that. Then she found some needle marks on his neck and the tox screen came back with some very nasty poison in his blood. So it's murder and our Chief Constable don't like that sort of thing on our patch so wants results yesterday."

Neil sighed "Sorry I can't be more help but I didn't really know him. Now I apologise for kicking you out but I have to go and pick up Ava from our Dragon friends."

"Give 'em my regards," said Howard as he left. " Our kids love a trip through the portal now and again. We are probably due to make a visit soon. We'll have to make it a joint one. Let me know if you hear anything on the grapevine."

Neil hurried along to the pithead lift and when the cage arrived stepped in closed the gate grill and pressed the button for the lowest level. When the lift shuddered to a halt he opened the cage and hurried across the cavern to the slab of striped rock and passed through as if it was mist, the only sensation a slight tingle from the carved wooden band on his left wrist. Stepping from the cave mouth into the evening pink sunshine of Dragon World he was just in time to see the squadron of dragons circle and glide down for a soft landing as he reached the end of the cliff path and stepped onto the springy purple grass.

The last to land was Golden Friend and Neil could hear the whoops of joy and greeting from his daughter leaning from her saddle as the dragon swooped over his head to land precisely by the lectern where Llewelyn stood with his stacks of scrolls. So exact was the golden dragon's touch down that not one of the scrolls was ruffled or displaced. Releasing the straps Ava jumped down from the dragon's back and rushed to her dad who scooped her up and hugged her tight.

"Had a good time then?" he said as she snuggled closer.

"Fantastic! We saw so many new things and I've got presents for you and Mum and Brassroyd and the cousins and the dogs and crows and all sorts of presents for me as well." Two of the dragons came across the grass towing a cart stacked with bags and sacks which they explained belonged to Ava and said they would take up the path and through the portal. A third Dragon followed with a large rectangular parcel wrapped in brightly coloured silk and tied with a contrasting silk ribbon. Neil lowered his daughter to the grass and the dragon handed the parcel to her.

"This is is for Llewellyn from the Temple Lions I must go and give it to him," she said and hurried over to the large red dragon holding out the parcel for him to take. She then rummaged in her shoulder bag and produced two bulky letters one in a gold envelope with a silver wax seal bearing the image of a Temple Lion and the other in a stiff white envelope with a red wax seal bearing the coat of arms of the Grand Council and was from their Ambassador to Imperial Host. The Red Dragon Bowed to the girl and thanked her formally as was the protocol when receiving a message from an official diplomatic courier. Neil had walked over to join them and Llewellyn looked up and beamed at him pointing to a small silver broach pinned to his daughter's lapel.

"Ava has been given the honour of becoming an official Diplomatic Courier. The Speeding Dragon insignia gives her free and fast passage anywhere in Dragon World and immediate entry to our embassies and into the presence of the Ambassador.

Neil was impressed and congratulated Ava who glowed with pride at the recognition that the Ambassador, a lady dragon had conferred on her. Neil thanked Golden Friend and the six other dragons who had formed Ava's escort for keeping her safe then followed the excited girl up the path to the portal.

When they arrived back at 7A Pudding Founder's Lane it seemed that everyone had come to greet her return. Outside a mele of dogs and crows surrounded Sprocket who was regaling them with his adventures in the land of The Imperial Dragons. Ava sorted out the presents for crows and dogs onto a large tray which she carried out for Sprocket to hand round then went back into the kitchen to do the same for the presents for the humans. Everyone admired her courier badge and the cousins were very envious.

Ava gave Brassroyd his present and the cousins crowded round to watch him carefully unwrap it. Victoria and Kate each claimed one of the silk ribbons which bound it and Gill was given the Temple Lion badge which had been pinned to the bow. The wrapping was red silk with large, round, white spots just like Brassroyd's favourite handkerchiefs. he carefully folded it and tucked it in the breast pocket of his jacket. His present was a large, square book with gold corners on the covers and a beautiful picture of a Temple Lion rearing up on its four hind legs, its talons spread, and breathing fire. It was in red gold and silver against a midnight blue background and the beast was highlighted with tiny gemstones that sparkled. He opened the cover and flipped through several lavishly illustrated pages the text of which was in handwritten Chinese characters with a translation in English at the bottom of each page. It was a complete guide to the animals and plants of the World of the Imperial Dragons and was signed on the inside of the front cover by Ken, Jes, and The Ambassador. The old man was overjoyed and had to remove his spectacles to dab away some tears with a spotted handkerchief, not his new silk one. There were smart black and gold, silk bound, five-year diaries for her Dad and uncle, and embroidered silk handbags for her Mum and Aunty Jill. Best of all though there was a table full of party food which the children fell upon with ravenous hunger. All too soon the sky faded to black and the stars began to wink. People said their goodbyes and departed on foot or through the portal in Ava's bedroom and it was time for bed.

The following day being Monday Ava took her collection of pictures and some of the presents the Temple lions had given her and the report she had compiled about the lions and the Imperial Host which she gave to her teacher who was so impressed she asked Ava to tell them all about it. She was a little hesitant, to begin with, but soon was well into her story and as she came to the end the bell rang for morning playtime. Outside she was mobbed by her classmates asking questions about where she had been and what she had seen. She had to be careful to make it seem a story from her imagination as her Dad had warned her to keep the existence of dragons and Dragon World secret.

When Neil reached his office he pulled out his file of contacts who dealt with rare and exotic metals and proceeded to ring them to see if any of them knew any details of what Herbert Oakwood Associates had been up to recently. After an hour or so of chat with some of the main dealers, a picture started to appear. the original Herbert Oakwood had been a scrap metal dealer back in the days of Queen Victoria who had made his name importing and exporting special steel products and supplying the iron and steel industry with quantities of metals such as chromium which were added to the molten steel to give particular properties. Herbert's son had expanded the scrap business during the Second World War and had made his fortune collecting scrap metal such as park railings and fancy wrought iron gates to feed the war effort. He had been so successful that he was awarded a knighthood for services to industry by the post-war Labour government. Unfortunately, a series of bad investments and love of owning and betting on racehorses had, by the time his son, the second Herbert Oakwood left university, reduced the family fortune to next to nothing. Shortly after the young Herbert joined the family his father died in a car accident while driving back from Doncaster races. Herbert took over the business and found to his horror that it was deep in debt and nearing bankruptcy. He threw caution to the wind and ventured into some high-risk deals with some Eastern Block states desperate for special metals to modernise their failing industries. Some of these deals were bordering on smuggling but the returns were high and in five years Herbert Oakwood Associates was as financially sound as a vault full of gold bricks and the go-to company for really rare metals and alloys. Still, with a nose for the high risk, high-profit deal Herbert sailed the wreck ridden waters on the edge of the international metal markets and became very rich.

Neil got the impression that many in the market, though envying Herbert's wealth, didn't consider him a safe pair of hands in which to invest and many would insist on payment upfront on any deal with him just in case. His orders were large and complex and if any of the big ones should go wrong Herbert could lose everything. Regarding his recent business, it had mainly been in trace metals used in the electronics and computing industries, particularly telecoms coming out of Asia and the Far East. Some of Neil's contacts wondered if one of these customers was pressuring him for unobtainable stocks as he had been scouring markets across the world for two particular metals that nobody seemed to have. Neil pulled up the last inquiry from H.O.A and saw that it matched the metals that others had mentioned. None of the contacts had any clue as to who the end-user could be. He wrote up his findings and sent them by email to Howard hoping that they might prove useful

Chapter 14   Invasion

The new day broke with fire and panic along the Western border of The People's Republic. Endless stretches of coiled barbed wire were vapourised along with watchtowers and checkpoints. Supply depots near the border were turned to smoking ruins and concentrations of military vehicles blazed in their shattered compounds. No word of these disasters reached the rulers of the country who were still in the self-congratulatory conclave of the Party Congress while their underlings either fled in panic or searched frantically for someone or something to blame which was more believable then flying monsters from the mists of time.

Lee Mi was glued to the real-time feeds from her satellites and drones monitoring the operation as the area of devastation doubled every hour. She had altered the attack plan of the strike drones to take out communication and power networks. The initial strikes had to leave no trace of where the attacks were coming from so the drones self-destructed at the end of their runs. Retrievable drones that could be returned to base, rearmed, and sent out again were sent in to sterilise the areas which had been isolated by the attacks. Her only problem was that the production and replacement of the single-use attack drones were not keeping pace with demand. Her acquisition team had managed to buy two of the main miners and refiners of the metals she needed but supply was still lagging and if they moved too quickly and aggressively then it would leave a paper trail which could lead back to her companies and it was not yet time for her to announce domination of her dynastic lands. It was, however, time to start moving her troops into the sterilised areas and begin to establish her rule over the conquered lands. She tapped her keyboard sending the signal via a hack-proof laser link to the invasion units.

Orders sent, Lee Mi left her office and, with her secretary Chan, made her way to the observation room of the summoning chamber.

The view through the volcanic crystal window showed a dozen bald-headed men in red and yellow robes ringing finger cymbals and singing a monotonous dirge. The shape of the summoning chamber funnelled the sounds they were making towards the large glowing hearth and the resonator wire in its pit behind.

Though the chanting had been going on since sunrise and it was now nearing noon Lee Mi had arrived in time to witness the culmination of the acolyte's efforts. Throughout the ceremony, the resonance of the wire had steadily increased and could now be felt as a deep reverberation within the rock walls and floor. As their voices swelled a silvery shimmer began to form above the glowing coals. Still, the monks chanted, alternately bowing and straightening in front of the hearth as the shimmering pulsed and expanded. The more they chanted the denser the sparkling cloud became and the wider it spread. Flashes of electrical discharge could be seen at its centre, which became larger and more frequent. Eventually, the cloud filled the chamber and the monks could only be distinguished as bobbing shadows within the mist. The glow from the hearth began to brighten followed by a blinding flash, and there in the hearth sat a huge black and silver dragon. Everything stopped. Everyone held their breath as the dragon raised its head till its horned head almost touched the roof of the chamber. It reared back and its body swelled as it inhaled. Seconds ticked by then the dragon's head swooped forward its mouth agape and with a deafening roar flame poured forth. Nothing could be seen through the crystal window except sheets of ravening fire. Then suddenly it stopped. Silence fell the only sounds were the clicks and crackle of cooling metal.

"They've all gone! The monks have vanished. The resonator wire has broken. The walls, floor, and hearth have melted." Words tumbled from the white-faced engineer as he stared in horror at the devastation on the other side of the crystal window.

Lee Mi smiled her cold smile. "Look, you fool! You are missing the one important thing. There, on the remains of the fire. See it?"

The others in the observation stared at where she was pointing. In the centre of the shambles, nestled in the bed of white-hot embers was a large egg.

Still smiling Lee Mi turned and left the room followed by her mute secretary.

Chapter 15 News Leaks

Stephanie Thompson was an aid worker for a small underfunded charity trying to fight sight loss in rice farming communities caused by a water-borne parasite. The tiny worm-like creature laid its eggs on the shoots of the plants which grew along the banks of the rice paddies. These plants were in turn eaten by the water buffalo the farmers used as their beasts of burdens and also to plough the soil before the paddies were flooded for planting. The parasites grew in the animal's gut and the adult worms were excreted by the buffalos to swim free in the flooded fields when the faeces dissolved. Anyone drinking or washing in the infected water would pick up the parasites which would enter the victim's bloodstream and make its way to the eyes where it would feed on the retina and optic nerve before emerging from the tear ducts to drop onto the ground and make its way to the plants and grasses to lay its eggs. The result for the unfortunate victim was total and incurable blindness.

The charity had perfected a vaccine that, when injected into an uninfected child or adult would create antibodies that would find the worms and kill them before they reached the eyes. The problem was convincing the uneducated population firstly that invisible worms from buffalo poo were causing the blindness and secondly that sticking needles into them and their children would do anything but hurt. Stephanie had spent the last six months in long conversations with everyone from the village headmen to individual mothers, trying to get them to believe that the story she was telling was serious and not the ravings of a mad white woman with too many strings of beads. Finally, she had managed to bribe six of the younger wives to let her vaccinate them and their children by offering boxes of baby milk formula. She had learned enough not to hand out the boxes till after mother and baby had been treated, so called over the first patient and took out the first single-use syringe from the insulated box. Carefully swabbing the area of skin with disinfectant she first injected the mother then the child. The little girl didn't even flinch, being more interested in a pair of small birds squabbling over a seed pod that had fallen from a nearby bush. Steadily Stephanie worked through the line of six adults and nine children handing each mother a box of baby formula before they left. As the last patient walked away she stood and stretched to relieve the stiffness in her back from bending over the infants. Rummaging in her bag she pulled out her new mobile phone to send a text report of her first successful clinic and switched it on. The scream from behind the wall of the shelter she had been using almost caused her to drop the phone and she ran around the end of the lean-to hut to see what the commotion was all about. A group of women and children and two old men were shouting and pointing away across the paddy fields at what appeared to be a black bat swooping down towards a group of people scattering in all directions. Only as she saw how small the running people were did she realise how huge the black bat must be. Stephany clicked on the phone's camera to video and pointed it towards the action. As she panned across following the silhouette of the bat a sheet of flame blossomed from the creature sweeping across the flooded fields as it banked and turned towards them. More fire shot from the beast as it closed the distance to where she was standing. Suddenly realising the danger she shouted at the petrified crowd breaking thee spell and as one they all ran and crouched behind the block wall of the shelter. Flame boiled across the compound and black shadow flashed over them. The beast turned again and flamed another line of fields and a line of telephone poles and wires which bordered them. Once again the beast arrowed across more fields following its twin lances of fiery destruction then it turned its nose upward, rapidly climbed a hundred or so feet, and disappeared in a flash of light and a thunderous bang. Except for the direct pass over the shelter, Stephanie had caught the complete incident on video. She walked around the end of the wall which had shielded them and gasped at what she saw. The blockwork wall had been heated to such a temperature it had fused into something like glass which had run and sagged like a thick liquid. She took more photos of this. As the villagers ran out into the fields to look for survivors Stephanie typed a quick text of what had happened and sent it to the charity. She also posted it on her Youtube page. then went to see if she could help the villagers.

Sitting in the rented two-room hovel she was using as her base later that night and working by the flickering light of an oil lamp Stephanie typed out a more detailed report to the head office of the charity in Manchester. The village had been very lucky. Though they had lost all their rice crop nobody had been killed. a few had lost their hair and some had small burns and blisters but the wounds were minor. A few miles away the local administrative centre had been raised to the ground with hundreds of casualties and over forty dead. The area had been isolated from the rest of the country as all power and phone lines had been cut. A call for help had been sent out on the only means available, a young boy with a moped who had just refilled his fuel tank with petrol and was riding back to his home several miles out of town when the dragon struck. It would be hours if not days before any help would reach the survivers.

Stephanie stared at the blank screen of the satellite connection unit which she used to get through to the UK on the many occasions when the power and phone lines went down, often because of something as mundane as a tree falling against the wires or a water buffalo relieving an itch by rubbing against a pole and pushing it over. She had known the day before that the battery was low but had been in too much of a hurry to plug in the charger. Now the connection had failed just as her message and video had gone out. It would take two hours of cranking the hand generator to get enough power back into the battery to re-establish the connection and she was already exhausted, it would have to wait till morning. Her saggy bed was far from comfortable but its siren call could be resisted no longer. She flopped fully clothed onto the blankets and drifted into a deep sleep with dreams haunted by black shadows in the sky and flames springing up where ever she turned.

She awoke, dripping with sweat as the sun began to clear the horizon. Stephanie groaned and stretched, then filled a pan with water and dropped in a coffee bag. It could not be put off any longer she would have to crank the generator. It could be days if not longer before the power came back on. She worked steadily till the water boiled and she lifted the pan of bitter coffee off the flame and poured it into the stained mug adding three spoons of sugar to improve the flavour. Taking a couple of sips she set the mug down by the generator and continued cranking. When the dregs of her second coffee had gone cold she had managed to get enough energy into the power cells for the satellite link to reconnect. Her phone immediately began to bleep and the first thing to appear on her screen was her Youtube video. Her eyes opened wide at the number of plays and shares. The figure was in the millions and climbing rapidly as she watched. There was a notification that several attempts had been made to take down the video but these had been overridden by the popularity of the piece. The phone began to ring and Stephanie answered the call to the frantic voice of her manager wanting to know if she was safe and uninjured. She managed to reassure the worried woman but said she had to cut the call to continue to crank the generator to get back to full charge. She assured her manager she would be back in touch later.

The phone on Lee Mi's desk buzzed. She answered it tersely. The head of the public relations company which handled all her company's press relations was calling to bring to her notice an item which was flooding the internet. His contract had a clause requiring his company to monitor all items including dragons and this was the biggest dragon news he had ever seen. He played the Youtube clip and asked for Lee Mi's reactions.

"Interesting. It is very well put together for a piece of fake news." she drawled. "Keep an eye on it and any related pieces. Thank you for bringing it to our attention. I cant see that we need to react to it in any way."

She replaced the receiver then immediately snatched it up again pressed the button to call her assistant and when he arrived issued a string of commands which would switch the attack and invasion into top gear. The calls and orders went out immediately and across the globe numerous organizations sprang into action.

Victoria waited by her Mum's car in the school car park while she went to collect her sister and brother from the middle school across the playing fields. She had moved to the upper school after her thirteenth birthday and now wore a tailored fawn jacket instead of the boxy navy blue ones her younger siblings had to put up with. They didn't seem to mind, but she had envied the older girls with their fitted garments for some time. Now she too was as stylish as anyone could be in a school uniform. Kate came running up the path beside the cricket and rugby pitches arriving red-faced and breathless.

"Did you bring your tablet with you this morning?" she gasped

Victoria rummaged in her shoulder bag and produced it flipping open the lid of the case.

"Whats the blazing rush?" she asked her sister who was breathing more normally at last.

"Open Youtube. Millie found a clip of huge black dragons burning up fields and people."

"It's probably a clip from 'Game of Thrones'. Said Victoria

"No! It's real. it was posted yesterday by an aid worker in China along with a report to her head office. The B.B.C. has picked it up and is running it on the news. We have to get to Dragon World and find out what's going on.

Victoria found the clip and watched open-mouthed as the huge black monster dropped from the skies breathing fire and destroying everything in its path.

"It can't be real, dragons don't do things like that." she pressed record and copied the clip to the hard drive. There was no internet on Dragon World and Golden Friend and Llewellyn needed to see this. If these were real dragons they had to be stopped before all their dragon friends were tarred with the same brush.

Their mother drove home carefully and calmly despite the exhortations from her daughters to put her foot down between explaining to their brother what all the fuss was about. As soon as they reached home they raced up to Kate's room and through the portal in the cupboard bursting into Ava's room to find their cousin busily colouring in a large picture of a Temple Lion in mid-dance.

Kate carefully pushed aside the pens and pencils while Victoria slapped down her tablet and punched keys to bring up the clip.

"You've got to see this now," said Kate as her sister pressed play. Gil craned to see the screen for his first view of the clip. The video ran silently as there was no soundtrack and the four watched in silence. As soon as it ended Ava pressed repeat and watched it through again.

"It can't be real," she said shaking her head. "We have to show Llewellyn and the others. Come on!" she jumped up grabbed her coat and the four children clattered downstairs. As they ran through the kitchen to the back door Ava called to her mother that they were going to see the dragons. Louise's voice followed them through the door telling them not to be long as she was making tea.

Neil met them as they ran into the Pitt yard and escorted them to the lift and down to the bottom level and the portal. he also followed them through and down the cliff path to the large red dragon who had been alerted by their calls as soon as the children had burst from the mouth of the portal cave.

Victoria placed the tablet on Llewellyn's lectern and pressed the play button. The four children were vibrating with impatience as Neil and the Red dragon watched the images on the small screen.

"That is very clever. It is some sort of TV show, yes?" thought Llewellyn

"No! It's real. It's been shown on the B.B.C News and they always check stuff before showing it." said Kate

"Then this is terrible! I must call the Grand Council to see this." the five humans stood in silence while the red dragon raised his snout to the sky, closed his eyes and concentrated hard. When he had finished he turned to the group.

"They are coming. Follow me to the library where we can put this on one of the big screens for all the Council to see."

Llewellyn placed his clawed hand on the surface of the black basalt slab and it slid back opening the entrance to the library, then moved over to one of the large flat tables. He pressed a talon into a series of indentations down one edge of the tabletop and two polished glass-like sheets rose from the surface.

"Place your device between the sheets please Victoria." She did as she was asked while the red dragon prodded some more indentations. A slab of polished white marble descended from the roof. shimmered for a few seconds then cleared to show a magnified picture of the tablet's screen.

"Now we must wait for the Council."

It could not have been five minutes before the first dragon entered the library and not more than ten before the last dragon, Golden Friend, hurried in and the door closed behind him. The lights dimmed and the clip started to play on the big screen. The Dragons played it through ten times pausing it in several places to study details.

"Most realistic. but not real dragons." Dagon heads nodded. " If a real dragon tried to fly like that its wings would break." again heads nodded. "The flame is wrong, it is too liquid and not hot enough. It burns too slowly" again nods and murmurs of agreement.

Llewellyn had been consulting screens on another table and rejoined the discussion.

"Whoever is behind this criminal hoax has done their research. The only reference to dragons being used as beasts of war relates to the early emperors and warlords of ancient China. These are not copies of the Imperial Host or the dragons would be red and gold. Their fire was also hotter and more spear-like used for aerial conflict. Ground attacks by Imperial Dragons were made by rending with their long and powerful back legs and claws.

There is however one reference to a very early dynasty, more bandits than true emperors, The Qin. These used specially bred, large black dragons, and these were widely used to ravage surrounding tribes and subdue enemies. The dynasty died out because the dragons they bred were particularly bad-tempered and had the habit of killing those who tried to train them. Also, this type of dragon only produced one egg every twenty years so replacing any animals killed in battle was a slow and dangerous business."

The discussion went back and forth between the various members of the council and looked as if it might go on all night. Neil moved quietly over to Llewellyn and whispered their apologies and asked him to let them out of the library so they could go back and get the children fed.

"Thank you for bringing these appalling events to our notice I will let you know the outcome of the Council's deliberations in due course." The red dragon watched as the humans made their way back towards the cliff path. He was just about to return to the library and the ongoing conference when a sleek young dragon dropped from the sky and skidded to a halt by the lectern.

"The courier is needed urgently." Came the young dragon's thought.

Llewellyn spun round and sent an urgent thought to the group who were only halfway up the cliff path. They all turned and looked to see the red dragon becoming them to return. Hurrying back to the lectern they were told that Ava was needed urgently at the Imperial enclave as the Temple Lions had a problem she needed to know about.

Llewellyn turned to Neil "Get the saddle and Ava's flying gear. She will show you where it is kept." He paused, head up, as he received a thought from elsewhere, "You three come with me. The Grand Council needs a closer look at the moving pictures and with our claws, we would wreck your device."

As Neil and Ava returned with the saddle and flying suit they saw the others following Llewellyn towards the library. They fastened the saddle onto the young dragon while he grabbed a quick meal to give him the energy for the return flight. Neil helped Ava put on the flying suit and made sure that the breathing hood was properly fixed. Then he lifted her into the saddle and checked the straps of the harness. He stepped back and the dragon, with his daughter crouched low in the saddle, leapt into the air and with a downward swoop of his wings climbed up towards the clouds.

Chapter 16   Are Dragons Real?

The President and leader of the Party finished his speech to a standing ovation from the delegates which went on and on as he bowed many times to all parts of the audience. He turned and walked slowly from the Hall of the People, pausing to shake hands with various of the senior officials who had also been seated on the main platform. The Congress of the People was over for another four years and the President sighed with relief as he took his seat in the sleek black limousine for the short journey back to the palace. He and his wife walked up the wide steps to the main doors of the building which were opened by the guards who snapped to attention and saluted smartly. They parted in the entrance hall his wife taking the lift to their private apartments while the president surrounded by numerous aids walked along to his office to start to catch up on the inevitable mountain of paperwork which would be waiting for him.

He had sorted the files into two piles, those from department heads and a thicker pile from the political officers, both official and secret within every branch of the government and military. The files from department heads he transferred unread to the out tray. They were worthless containing only what the bureaucrats thought he wanted to see and skipping over or missing out any bad news. The President picked up the first political file marked Crop Yields. the reports were dated from the week before the Peoples Congress where the minister for Food Production had delivered a glowing speech about the success of the collective farms in feeding the population. These files told a different story of targets missed, rat-infested food stores, failed deliveries, and corruption leading to local food shortages and discontent in the population. Pressing a button on the small recording device he dictated a series of memos that would shake up local food depots and lead to the dismissal and imprisonment of corrupt officials. He pressed a second button sending the messages to the Office of the Political Commissars for immediate action. The next file was marked State Security and covered reports on the Army, Navy, Airforce, and security services. The most recent of these reports were less than a day old and at the top of the pile, some bright young analysts had collated a series of seemingly unrelated snippets from the Western borders regarding the loss of power and communications with checkpoints. Each report was, on its own insignificant but the analyst had attached a map linking the various blackouts which encircled thousands of hectares of territory all along the border provinces and pushing well into the country. Quickly skimming the rest of the papers he realised that none of the regional commanders or their staff had picked up on this and no action had been taken to investigate what was happening. He dictated a string of commands that would scramble aircraft to overfly the region and send two light armoured and mobile infantry columns into the country to report from the ground. This done he continued to plough through the pile of folders while he waited for reactions to come in.

Sergeant Pilot Lee Gin Tang was dozing in the cockpit of his fighter bomber at the end of the runway. His navigator/gunner in the front seat was flipping through the readiness reports.

"I hope we don't get a scramble, we have only fifty percent ammunition, no bombs, just two missiles, and seventy percent fuel load so if we lift off we'll be flying with our pants around our ankles. Oh and we only have two packs of defence flares." the navigator's voice crackled over the internal communications circuit.

"Great! nothing like being fully prepared for disaster. When will the stores get a full complement of spares and fuel? Let us hope the filthy capitalists are selling off even more of their spare parts than our corrupt high ups are. Otherwise, we are in deep trouble if we need to bump heads."

He had just flipped the coms switch when the cockpit alarm began to howl and his instruments flashed red.

"Me and my big mouth," he muttered as the ground crew rushed to fire up the engines and the double cockpit began to close. Within seconds he had the all-clear from the crew chief, had checked off the breaks, and was rolling as the engines built to their full screaming power for takeoff.

As the wheels left the runway Gin pulled the joystick hard back and the plane rocketed upward on full afterburner. The navigator was muttering altitude and course information in his headphones as he levelled off and pointed the fighter toward the western horizon.

"What on Earth had lit a fire under control's backside?" asked the navigator.

"Your guess is as good as mine. What are our orders?"

"To overfly the Western boarder from checkpoint Delta to checkpoint Romeo and seventy kilometres inland all the way up. We are to report anything unusual and take recon pictures of anything we see."

"You better get Control to scramble the Recon Bird We have no camera on board," said Lee, grinning at the embarrassment that would cause among the brass hats.

For the next fifteen minutes, they flew toward the border. Lee had throttled back to conserve fuel and give the Recon Bird a chance to get in the air and catch up with them. The sky was clear and so was the radar though there was a haze to the west which could be smoke. They would be coming up on their search area in another three minutes. Suddenly the target lock warning started to warble.

"We are being painted by a S.A.M battery twenty kilometres ahead and to starboard." said the navigator.

"Probably bored and using us for targeting practice," answered Lee

"Damn! No! Missile lock and launch. The idiots have fired on us.

Lee slammed open the throttles, released two decoy flares and pulled the nose up to out climb the missiles. Their surface to air missiles didn't have a long burn and his aircraft could outpace them anyway.

"Another launch. Six missiles. Those aren't ours either, they're closing too fast and they ignored the decoys." screamed the navigator.

Lee threw the aircraft into a series of frantic twists as the first missile missed them and exploded in front and to port. The second didn't miss and hit the tail fin shearing it off like a hot knife through butter.

"Eject!" ordered Lee and was conscious of the explosion as both cockpit canopies cleared and he and the navigator were shot from the doomed plane He punched the harness release and pulled the ripcord and felt the hard tug as the parachute opened. he glanced down just in time to see his plane obliterated as the six remaining missiles hit.

Chapter 17 Beware Angry Mothers

The young dragon was fast and Ava kept her head down below the screen of the saddle. When she occasionally popped up to see the view ahead the wind was so strong it made her neck ache. After five hours crouched in the saddle Ava's legs were beginning to cramp and she was very relieved when her mount dropped his left wing and spiralled down to a mountain pasture. It took Ava's cramped fingers longer than she wished to unbuckle the harness and even more time for her stiff legs to cope with climbing down from the dragon's back. While she walked back and forth to stretch her legs the dragon unpacked food packs from pouches strapped to its chest. They ate quickly and while the dragon repacked his pouches Ava lengthened the boot stirrups on the saddle and locked them in place so that she would be safe if she dozed off. All too soon they were back in the air.

"How much longer before we reach the Embassy?"

"About another three hours."

Ava groaned but there was nothing she could do about it so she tightened her straps and locked her hood to the headrest of the saddleback, closed her eyes, and was soon asleep.

It seemed that she had barely closed her eyes when a feeling of falling snapped her wide awake. The dragon was in a steep dive and as they broke through the cloud base she saw the Embassy below. As they came into land two Temple Lions galloped across the lawn to meet them. To Ava's delight, it was Ken and Jes.

"No time to waste. The Ambassador will see you on your return. Climb aboard." Said Ken holding open what appeared to be a papoose attached to his chest. With one smooth move, he lifted Ava from the saddle and slid her into the pouch pulling the drawstring up, leaving only her head still covered in its breather hood showing. Immediately the two Lions set off at a gallop.

At first, Ava was face down and had to bend her neck back to see where they were going but this proved uncomfortable so she slid down inside the pouch and rolled onto her back. The Lions ran on their six legs and the gentle rocking motion soon had Ava dozing off.

In no time she was roused by Jes's thought.

"Wake up sleepy head we're almost there."

Ava emerged from the pouch and Ken raised his upper body to give her a view of the approaching city. She could see a towering pall of smoke and steam rising from where the temples were located.

"What's going on?" she asked

"First put these on." thought Ken handing her a pair of large earmuffs. You will need them to cut out the sound of the monks chanting or you will be fast asleep and see nothing."

Ava freed her arms from the pouch and pulled on the earmuffs. As they neared the Temple the first thing she noticed was the absence of guard Lions at the gate.

"Where are the guards?" she thought

"Ken and I were on guard but were sent to collect you." Answered Jes.

Passing through the gate the Lions climbed the steps leading to the temple forecourt. The sight that was revealed was the source of the flames and smoke.

A large, black and silver dragon was pinned to the ground by a pile of singed and blackened Temple Lions. The dragon was struggling and belching out gouts of flame and steam but as fast as it shook a lion off another took its place. The struggle was surrounded by a double ring of monks who were busy bowing and chanting though Ava couldn't hear them because of the earmuffs. She could, however, see their mouths moving and see many of them clashing finger cymbals and banging gongs.

"The dragon is an Imperial Female and she is livid because she has lost her egg. Unless she is calmed and taken into the hatching room she could go mad and burn down the entire city." This thought came from Jes.

"How did she lose the egg?" asked Ava again being thankful for thought communication as with the obvious sound and fury going on she was sure that no words would have been audible.

"She was coming to the Temple to lay her egg in the hatching hearth which is kept white-hot to help the embryo to grow and mature. On her way, she disappeared for about five minutes and when she reappeared she was furious, thrashing about and incinerating anything in sight." Thought Ken.

"The Brood squad was called out and set about trapping and smothering her while the monks started the calming chant. It may appear to be more like a battle than bedtime but it is working. There are only half as many Lions as it took to pin her down at first and she is not flaming nearly as much. We were lucky she was in the Temple grounds when it happened if she had been flying free the entire city would have been burning." Jes grinned nervously and Ken added " We have a saying, 'Come between a mother and her egg on pain of Death'. It is a situation nobody would willingly place themselves in."

The two lions skirted around the continuing struggle and entered the Temple through a side door. Ken helped Ava from the pouch and the trio walked along a corridor and into a large circular room. A very old monk in scarlet and gold robes was studying a long strip of paper protruding from an ornate machine on which some pens on sprung arms twitched and jiggled. The paper beneath them unrolled steadily and this produced graphs of different colours on the strip.

The ancient monk looked up and beckoned them to look at the wavering lines. Most of them were almost straight showing only tiny variations, but one coloured deep purple ranged wildly across the strip.

"That one is a resonator." Thought Ken "That is a summoning happening. There hasn't been one of those in centuries, not since the last Emperor died. No wonder the female disappeared. She was drawn into another dimension and the shock must have caused her to lay her egg. We may never find it and if that's the case she will pine and fade away. This is tragic."

" Is there no way to trace the egg?" thought Ava. "Can't Seeker dragons find it?"

"They may be able to but we have no Seekers here."

"Can you get me something with the mother's scent on? Then I could take it back with me and set the Seekers to hunt."

Jes brightened up. "I will go to the mother's roost and fetch something for you to take back." And she rushed out of the room.

"That was good thinking Ava. We need to find the egg before it hatches or people may be killed. Baby Imperials are even more bad-tempered than their mothers and will flame anyone or anything that comes near them. Great patience and well-insulated armour are needed to train a War dragon," mused Ken. "Climb into the pouch and we will return to the embassy. Jes will meet us there and you can speak with the Ambassador while we wait for her."

Ava made herself comfortable and they set out on the return journey. Passing the Temple forecourt Ava watched the now sleeping dragon being pushed and pulled onto a large, low trolley to be moved into the hatchery. The monks were still chanting so she was glad that she had not removed the earmuffs. Finally, she could relax as the Lions smooth running action ate up the distance towards the mountains.

The meeting with the Ambassador didn't take long. She had a packet of reports ready for Ava and added another after the girl had told her what had happened to the female dragon. By the time she emerged from the embassy, Jes had arrived with a padded package containing dragon bedding sealed in a porcelain jar. The courier dragon was ready and Jes checked Ava's flying suit while Ken adjusted the saddle and tightened the straps on the packages.

"It should be a quick trip. You'll have a strong tailwind all the way," Ken told her as he lifted her into the saddle and tightened her harness. Then it was up and away, hardly giving Ava time to wave and shout goodbye.

Howard and Neil sat in Neil's office in the pithead yard deep in discussion of what information had been turned up on Herbert Oakwood Associates. Two half-empty mugs of coffee which had gone cold some time previously stood to one side while the rest of the surface of the large old desk was covered with cardboard folders and papers.

"Having followed up on all the leads your phone calls turned up, things started to point to the Far East. Several large electronics firms in India and South Korea and some shell companies in Singapore and Hong Kong were pinpointed. The Indian police were quite helpful but without hard evidence, they couldn't get warrants to raid offices.

The police in South Korea were more proactive and hacked the computer systems of suspect companies. Their geeks didn't even need to set foot on the companies property. The boys in Singapore dug up some very dodgy deals but when it came to Hong Kong and anything pointing to the Chinese mainland the Communists snapped shut like giant clams." said Howard. He sorted through the papers and pulled together several sheets and a handfull of files.

"Look at these. Though most of these companies head up as manufacturers of everything from televisions to cars and medical equipment every one of them has an advanced avionics division and any of the orders for rare metals we have been able to track back to the source has led to one of these special units. Their security is tighter than a drum but we did follow one delivery, no idea what it contained, to a cosmetics company on the American/Canadian border.

Now I know that the business of making ladies pretty is huge and cutthroat but this mob has security on a level which makes your average arms manufacturer look like it's living in a clear glass bubble. Our finance guys have tried to work out their company structure but have run into brick walls and blind alleys wherever the went. Holding companies within shell companies, private offshore offices, one tax haven after another. Qin-T-Sential, that's the name of the organisation hasn't paid a penny of tax in any country in the world. They have offices in most major cities but they're just fronts. One of our plain clothes ladies went into their London office posing as a buyer for one of the big mail-order catalogues. She sat in their plush reception area till a smooth young man in a sharp suit came out of a lift and escorted her into another lift which went up five floors and opened into a showroom full of display cabinets and glossy photos of models wearing the company's products.

They discussed ranges, inspected branding and packaging. She was presented with a very refined case containing a pile of cosmetics and brochures then escorted down in the lift and shown out. No sign of a factory, no trace of anyone other than the receptionist, who appeared to do nothing but paint her nails and answer the occasional phone call, and the smart young man. Observation of the building has only seen those two enter and leave the premises. All the other offices are accessed through a second reception at the back and none have anything to do with cosmetics or health foods. It appears to be a complex with nothing at the middle and no routes in."

"Well, thanks for the update, now I must get through the portal to fetch Ava. She should be back by now."

As he emerged from the portal cave Neil saw the children coming out of the library followed by a group of dragons who, one by one took to the air and flew off in different directions. By the time he reached the bottom of the cliff path, only Llewellyn and Golden Friend remained with the children who all began to talk at once. Neil put his hands over his ears to cut out the din while the red dragon brought him up to date by thought. He thanked the dragons then ushered the still babbling quartet up the cliff path and home for tea.

Chapter 18 Progress on Some Fronts

Stephanie groaned as she rolled out of her rock hard bed. She had spent the last two days providing first aid to a never-ending queue of survivors. Anything from minor cuts and bruises to broken arms and legs and burns of varying severity. No help had arrived and when the teenager returned pushing his moped he reported that everywhere for miles around was the same. Buildings, crops, and checkpoints burned to ash. No power, no telephones, and no sign of the army or police.

A commotion outside drew her attention and she opened the door of the shed she called home, to see what was happening. The villagers were lined up and being loaded into one of several trucks painted in shades of grey and brown camouflage which matched the colours of the uniforms of the dozen or so troops who were herding the civilians onto the transport. She called out to one of the soldiers in Mandarin and he turned to face her, waving at her with a crowd control baton, signalling for her to join the queue by the truck and shouted a command in a language Stephanie didn't understand. She tried again this time in English.

"Get on truck now!" came the reply in heavily accented English.

"I must get dressed," she replied and turned back to the shack. The soldier ran over and grabbed her arm.

"On truck now!" he shouted and dragged her over to the tailboard of the truck. Two of the other soldiers lifted her up and threw her into the truck and when she grabbed the tailboard to try and get up her fingers were rapped hard with a baton and she fell back as others were bundled in. Before she could right herself the truck started off and several of the villagers fell on top of her. By the time she had crawled from under the struggling bodies and was able to see out of the back of the vehicle, they were half a mile from the village from which smoke and flame were rising and the truck was going too fast to risk jumping off. Stephany slumped back and shuffled over to lean against the flapping canvass cover. What could she do now? Nobody would know where she was and her only link with the outside world was probably at the centre of the smoke and flames receding in the distance. To her shame, she gave in and burst into tears burying her face in her hands. The stunned peasants around her just sat and stared at the flapping canvas with unseeing eyes.

The Grand Council of Noble Dragons had been in session all night and as the new day dawned they came to an agreement. The insult to dragon kind must be stopped and the false dragons must be wiped out before the destruction that was happening on the Human world spread to their world. Seekers would be sent out to locate portals as close as possible to the seat of the trouble and to locate the missing egg. A force of dragons would be selected to go through the portal and put a stop to these upstarts. Messengers were sent out.

The President was rapidly losing his temper. It was over two hours since the order to scramble the Border Protection squadrons had been given and not a word had come through from the Air Ministry. He had not expected any news from the army it would be at least another three hours before the light armoured divisions would reach the Western Border and be in a position to report back, But the damn Pilots should be seeing something by now and sending back photography that the analysts could look at. He angrily jabbed one of the buttons on his phone and was immediately put through to the head of the airforce.

"What's Happening! Your planes should have reported in by now?"

"I am sorry Mr President. We sent out two of the rapid response fighter bombers but both have failed to report in. A high altitude reconnaissance plane has been refuelled in flight and is on its way from the Rusian border. We have also scrambled a ground attack squadron which should be in the area any time soon."

"Not good enough! Response times like this could have armoured columns approaching the capital before you fools have fallen out of bed. Go to full alert immediately and saturate that area.

The Attack Controller reported that a storm front had moved in covering the entire area with thick cloud so the high-level recon plane was returning to base as neither of its cameras even with infra-red could penetrate the clouds and the radar wasn't picking up anything useful either.

The ground attack squadron was ordered in, its air cover fighters were to remain above the clouds to deny the airspace to any enemy aircraft. Below' the lead fighter/bomber broke from the cloud base and ran straight into a missile from the battery which had tracked it throughout its approach. The explosion fragmented the plane even before the crew could react. Two more aircraft dived from the low cloud, the first meeting the same fate as the lead craft. The second was enveloped in a boiling cloud of fire that stripped the metal skin from the wings in a flash. With no lift or means of control, the plane continued its plunge straight into the ground. Seconds after impact a single ejector seat exploded from the crater to crash down ten metres away. The parachute failed to open and the occupant was already dead. None of the remaining planes fared any better and an area of twelve hectares was dotted with randomly spaced smoking craters.

Lee Mi watched the steady spread of the line surrounding the captured territory. In less than three days, her forces had taken nearly three-quarters of the territory once ruled by her ancestors. The Government of the People was playing right into her hands. The usual blanket of news suppression had snapped into place and that combined with her own jamming of all radio and radar, and the destruction of all telephone lines and cell phone towers meant that Government forces were blind, with no idea what was going on. The storm front with its blanket of dense low cloud was an unexpected natural ally, though her people had tracked its approach and prepared for the conditions it might bring. She smiled her cold smile and went back to dealing with the day to day running of her global business empire.

Chapter 19 Flags are Raised

In a small plain office somewhere in Whitehall a thin man in a grey suit took off his glasses, rose from his chair, and walked the four steps to the tall narrow window which looked out onto a plain weathered stone wall opposite. He raised his arms above his head and stretched, several of the joints of his narrow frame clicked. He walked back to his desk replaced his black-rimmed spectacles and stared again at the five sheets of paper placed neatly on the leather inset of the desktop. Something was going on in China. The reports were just snippets of longer ones and at first glance seemed unrelated He had studied the intricacies of the communist state for decades and was now an expert in reading between the lines. The Congress of the People had just finished and he had been prepared for the usual mountain of blustering hype and massaged statistics but within twelve hours all the usual sources had gone quiet. Nothing was coming over the wires, no gossip from the embassies, nothing second hand from the North Koreans or Vietnamese. Something bad was happening and he wanted to uncover it before it exploded in everyone's face. He picked up the phone and made a number of rapid calls then frowned scooped up the papers, locked them in a drawer then left his office and descended several flights of stairs to the basement where the satellite feeds were analysed. He passed the European screens and those covering the Near East then paused by the main China feed. The girl at the screen, sensing his presence lifted one side of the headphones off her ear and turned to face him.

"What can I do for the Puzzles desk today?" she asked with a smile

He returned the smile acknowledging the nickname that everyone used for his one-man operation.

"Anything unusual? Troop movements? Aircraft, anything like that? Its all gone very quiet behind the bamboo curtain and that makes my skin crawl."

She turned back to her screen and pressed some keys. The image changed, zooming in on one of the main cross country routes.

"We noticed this. Its a column of mechanised infantry with light armoured support heading West." The image moved again further South "And here's another one moving North West which looks as if they should join up about here." Again the picture changed, zooming out to show the area towards the country's Western border. She circled a large area of cloud along a deepening area of low pressure.

"There has been some aircraft activity around this depression but the cloud plays havoc with the satellites we can't track a thing through that lot. Let me see if I can bring up the history of overflights for the last two days." Her fingers danced across the keys and a column of words and numbers appeared down the left side of the screen.

"Interesting." he murmured "How many airfields in that area?"

Again the girl typed and a series of red dots appeared on the map.

"Notice anything?" he asked

"There are no airfields in the cloud area. Why did you want to know?"

"Because if you look at the flight history more planes have entered that cloud than have come out. In fact, twice as many have gone in as have come out. So either there is a major field we don't know about or there are a lot of crashed planes under that cloud and nobody is making a fuss about it. Keep a close eye on that area and also both sides of the border. Please let me know if you spot anything or the cloud starts to break up and we can see the ground."

"Will do Sir," she said as he turned and strode out of the basement. He took the stairs two at a time bounding up them like a gazelle. Those who knew him maintained that never using the many lifts was what kept him stick thin.

He entered the large open plan office of the Far East station, six floors up from the basement, not at all out of breath, and as cool as if he had just left the chair in his office. Making straight for the desk of the head of station he dropped into the chair in front. The head of station looked up from the file he'd been reading.

"What brings Puzzles to me and what service can we provide for you?" asked the senior intelligence officer raising an eyebrow.

"How many assets have we got on our side of China's western border?"

"Not sure precisely, why?"

"There's a cold front along a large part of it with enough thick cloud to blind our satellites and more planes are going in than coming out. Before you ask there are no known airfields in the area and neither the Airforce or the Party high-ups are making any fuss about it. Add that to sightings of two columns of mechanised infantry with light armour support heading West and my instincts start to itch. I want as many eyes as possible on-site and some across the border if possible though I'm expecting the area to be in total lockdown."

Head of Station didn't ask silly questions he had known this man for long enough that when Puzzles smelled a rat it should be taken seriously. He picked up his phone and issued a section red alert with constant updates to be sent for his attention and immediate copy to Puzzles. With that, the two shook hands and the thin man went back to his office. One of the clerks had just brought in a tray with a teapot cup, saucer, milk, one plain biscuit, and no sugar when his phone rang. It was the Head of Station.

"Listen to this." there followed a recording of a radio message stating that the area was in total lockdown by non-Chinese troops. He had been close enough to hear them speak in what he thought was Mongolian but had had to retreat ten miles because of severe radio jamming coming out of China. He had seen widespread fire damage but no sign of Chinese soldiers or any civilians. Hectares of what had been rice paddies nearing harvest were just ash and blackened cracked mud.

The head of station came back on the line. "What the hell is going on out there? I've been on to the Yanks but even their high viz birds can't penetrate the murk. One of their infra-red birds did spot several hot impact craters well inland from the border but they can't raise any of their assets in the area because of blanket jamming. The Foreign Secretary has sent for the Chinese ambassador as it seems we have a British medical charity operating on that patch and their HQ can't raise their person out there. I don't suppose the Ambassador will do anything but flannel and stall, but we can't do much without a direct request for help from the Chinese leadership and you know how likely that is. As it's three in the afternoon on a Friday, nothing is going to happen till mid-morning Monday at best." The phone call ended.

Neil was just clearing his desk to go and meet Ava from school when reception rang through to say that two policemen wanted to speak to him.

"Is one of them very tall and black?" he asked and when the answer was yes he began to relax. "Send them through." he put down the phone then picked it up again and dialled Brassroyd's number. "Can you pick up Ava? It looks like I might be late leaving."

Brassroyd happily agreed and said that Sprocket had been fussing to see Ava all afternoon so it might solve two problems at once.

As Neil put down the phone there was a knock on his office door and Howard and a plainclothes officer were shown in.

"This is Inspector Packwood of the Serious Fraud Office," said Howard as Neil waved the visitors to comfortable chairs and his secretary came in with mugs of tea and a plate of chocolate biscuits. The inspector smiled, picked up one of the mugs, helped himself to two biscuits, and asked Howard to bring Neil up to speed with what had been happening.

"As you know the body at Black Top caused quite a stir locally and we flagged it up on the national computer as with all serious crimes. The link with Herbert Oakwood Associates rang a bell with Inspector Packwood who deals mainly with money laundering and corporate fraud. Also, the international links with the Far East and also Qin-T-Sential raised flags on the corporate tax avoidance team, so he made contact and asked if he could come up and speak to us. I think you'd better take it from here Inspector."

Swallowing the last of his biscuit and washing it down with a swig of tea, the Inspector began.

"The miraculous resurrection of Herbert Oakwood from financial disaster seemed too good to be true which is why he showed up on my radar. However, to date, the only thing we have been able to prove was that he was an extremely lucky man. He has for years dealt in the murkier end of the rare metals market but despite associating with many very shady customers he has managed to remain squeaky clean. always paying tax on his declared business deals and having clean records and financial statements to back up his business. It's his lifestyle which raises questions. Herbert junior has expensive tastes. He likes fast cars and equally fast women who are very high maintenance. All of this is paid for in cash and leaves no paper trail which is why we have been keeping an eye on him waiting for him to make a mistake. His untimely death allowed us to raid his offices and sweep them clean before any of his expensive team of lawyers and accountants could tie up loose ends and bury any evidence too deep to find. As a result, we have found some very suspicious dealings going on in and around the international metals market. Several leading dealers have recently had financial problems and been rescued and absorbed by a shadowy backer with no traceable assets. In-depth investigations have uncovered that all the problems and takeovers had links to the types of metals and alloys which Howard and his colleagues have been looking into and we are looking to merge our investigations."

There was a knock on the door and Neil's secretary put her head in to say that his daughter and her friends were asking for him.

"Excuse me for a moment. I won't be long," he said rising from his chair and making for the door. When he reached the reception area four excited children and what appeared to the receptionist to be a rather strange looking small dog were waiting for him.

We need to go through to see our friends." said Ava looking pointedly at the strange dog.

Neil understood immediately that she was referring to the dragons as he could see the dog for what it really was, namely Sprocket.

"Take them another brew through will you? I won't be long sorting this crew out." Neil said to the receptionist as he herded the children out into the yard and across to the lift.

"I'll have to put a stool in here so you can reach the buttons for yourselves. Then you won't need to mither me every time Sprocket brings you a message. I think that at least Victoria is old enough to be trusted by now to take you through the portal." He waved away the protests from the other three and pressed the button for the lowest level. The lift started down.

By the time the Fearsome Four and Sprocket reached the bottom of the cliff path, a small group of very senior and serious dragons was gathered around Llewellyn's lectern. The red dragon stepped forward to meet the children.

"We have combed our records and have found a link to these attacks. Long ago the part of your world you call China was controlled by a very warlike tribe called the Qin. Their military leaders are said to have ridden into battle on huge black dragons and used them to burn their enemies. This seems to match with what appears to be happening at present, both in the method of attack and the area in which the destruction is taking place. We have set a team of Seeker dragons searching for portals through to that part of your world and when we find a suitable route we will take action to stop the troubles. In the meantime, we have put our findings along with maps in these scrolls which you can take to your adults so they can find the wrongdoers in your world and bring them to justice." Llewellyn paused and handed the scrolls to Ava. "You, as an official messenger of the Grand Council must carry these messages." Ava accepted the scrolls and bowed to the group of dragons. Victoria stepped forward.

"What can the rest of us do to help to track down and fight these bandits?" she asked. "We can't just hang around while the grownups have all the fun."

There were nods of heads among the dragons and some fang-filled smiles. Golden Friend handed another scroll to Victoria.

"In there you will find a copy of the main facts we have prepared for Ava to take to her father. I am sure that between you and with the help of Bird Watch you may be of great help in tracking down the villains and bringing them to justice. You may need to speak to Dave at the museum as he has some clever machines to help gather the evidence." The grins these thoughts brought to the faces of the children held almost as many teeth as a dragon smile, so they thanked the members of the Grand Council, bowed deeply to each dragon in turn then hurried back up the cliff path to the portal cave.

SuddenlyAva shouted "Stop!" and ran back to the dragons.

" What about the missing egg?" she asked

"Another group of Seekers are searching for that and concentrating their efforts on the same area. We hope for news soon. We will send word as soon as we know something for sure." Thought Llewellyn.

"Thank you." She thought and ran back to catch up with the others.

Chapter 20 Bird Watch

As the children came out of the pithead lift they saw Neil waving goodbye to Howard and another man driving out of the gates of the yard. They hurried across to him bursting with ideas to help with the problem of dragon attacks. Hearing their approach Neil turned towards them.

"Ah, just the people I need to talk to. I want you to get-"

"Bird Watch!" the children chorused.

"Yes, exactly. How did you guess?" asked Neil in surprise.

The babble of replies was more than he could cope with, so he herded them into his office and ordered tea and biscuits all round while he untangled the countless strands of information they had brought him.

After an hour of discussion and planning a course of action had been sketched out and the meeting broke up leaving Neil to phone Howard and Inspector Packwood while the Fearsome Four scampered off to start putting their plan into action.

In his office in Whitehall, the man in the grey suit was sifting through a pile of files that had been gathered from various government departments and several of London's important museums which had collections of material on Chinese history. As he worked a pattern began to appear. The area of China that he was interested in corresponded almost exactly to the country once controlled by a group of warlords who call themselves the Qin dynasty. Also from the historical and folklore material was emerging a picture of merciless fighters who rode into battle on huge black dragons. None of these folk myths could be treated as fact but they did have strong connections with the stories which were beginning to leak across the border to the agents working for the Far East Station. His main problem was that there was no firm evidence to back up any of the frankly weird tales that were in the reports landing on his desk. He sat back in his chair stretching to relieve the ache in his back from hours of reading countless reports. He needed on-site informants, but where could he turn to get them. He stared at the ceiling for some moments then reached for the phone and dialled a Hereford number which didn't appear in any public directory.

The voice that answered was that of his nephew, a Major in a branch of the army which was rarely referred to, and its operations never discussed.

"What can I do for my favourite Uncle?" the major asked.

"I was wondering if any of your chaps were wandering about the Western borders of China at the moment?"

"Ah, this dragon business I suppose? Unfortunately, we have been told to keep well clear, but, I could put you in touch with a very useful bunch of civvies who will probably be far more useful as long as you don't go prying into the background of where the information comes from. I'll give you a name and phone number but don't make contact till I have spoken to them." The information was given and the phone went dead.

Nothing else happened till after lunch. His phone buzzed and his secretary said that she had a man from up north on the line who said that he had been asked to call by the Major.

"Put him through."

The call didn't take long and when it finished he asked his secretary to book him a seat on the first train to Leeds the next day and to e-mail the details to an email address he gave her. Being quite used to receiving cryptic instructions with no background information she did as asked and as soon as the tickets arrived the man in the grey suit collected them and muttering about being away for a day or two left the office early.

Gil was deep in conversation with the crows. He needed a blanket coverage of several addresses in the UK, around the clock watch on a rock off the coast of China, and any contact that could be made with a particular part of the West of China. He explained what needed to be looked for in each case and asked for the information to be fed back to his sisters who would write it up for people to read. Blaggard, the head of the Crow family allocated tasks to each of his three offspring. The three young crows, Faithless, Shiftless, and Dodger. took off to carry their messages to other birds and thence across land and sea to where Bird Watch would spring into action.

Across Great Britain birds sat on window sills, chimneys, roof beams of factories watching and listening. On and around a rocky pinnacle off the coast of China many gulls and other sea birds were taking more than a passing interest in the doings of the humans who lived on and in the rock. In the cloud shielded part of Western China, birds of all shapes and sizes noted and reported even the things which modern electronic monitoring could not pick up, and gradually all these reports filtered back to a stone house in a North country village where three girls duly noted them down. Nobody noticed the increase in bird activity around certain buildings and areas of countries but the birds noted everything and followed certain trucks leaving places and tracked them to their destinations.

The man in the grey suit boarded his train to the North and whiled away the journey reading newspapers and various files from his very secure briefcase. He stepped down from the train at Leeds City Station and was met at the barrier by a taxi driver and shown to a car in the rank outside. As soon as he was seated the car wound its way out of the city to the East/West motorway and on leaving this headed up into the high fells, finally arriving at the Pithead Yard in Batherby Bridge.

Neil met the taxi as it arrived, paid the driver, and after supplying a much-needed mug of restorative tea accompanied the man to his office. They spent the next two hours going through the dragon scrolls and the pile of information which Bird Watch was providing. The grey-suited man wondered where all this information and the very professional analysis came from particularly the obviously handwritten scrolls. He passed comment on this but Neil simply said that all would become clear before long. Following the second mug of tea, Neil accompanied the man to the mine lift and down to the lowest workings. They stepped out into the large cavern with the striped rock wall and Neil grasped the man's arm and walked towards the rock wall. Having been warned, over tea and biscuits, what would happen, the man in the grey suit didn't hesitate as Neil, slightly ahead of him, merged into the rock and simply followed him. He wasn't surprised to find himself in another cave or, when he stepped into the red sunlight, on the cliff path. His step did falter a little on seeing the two huge dragons waiting by a lectern on the purple grass at the base of the path. He followed Neil off the path and onto the grass keeping two steps behind as they approached the dragons.

"Welcome to Dragon World." The man in the grey suit flinched as the calming thought entered his brain. The whole feeling was so non-threatening that he began to relax and the dragon, sensing his unease, refrained from smiling.
" If you want to communicate with either of the dragons simply think what you wish to say and they will pick up your thoughts.

They don't read minds but just respond to thoughts directed to them." Neil explained.

"We have refreshments laid out on the table over there." thought the red dragon pointing to a tented structure with a table piled with food and two chairs made for humans.

"We have found from experience that a little food and drink put people at their ease, especially when they see that dragons don't eat humans." Llewellyn almost smiled at his little joke but managed to stop himself just in time. The mention of eating people accompanied by the sight of the number of fangs in a dragon smile could have proved too much.

"Neil has brought you here so you can see Dragon World for yourself. Believing that dragons exist without actually meeting them is rather more than most people can cope with. This is why your nephew didn't try to explain though we have worked with him and his troops on several occasions." thought the red dragon.

While they at and drank the two dragons explained about their connection with the people at 7 Pudding Founders Lane, the children, birds and dogs who made up the special relationship. They also gave some background to the connection with the S.A.S. in which his nephew served. It was also explained why so few people knew about dragons, after all, everyone accepted that they were myths, so talking about meeting dragons would mark one down as a credulous fool.

The man spent the next three days with the dragons usually accompanied by one of the children. Seeing how relaxed they were with the terrifying beasts reassured him.

When he returned to his office he carried with him a parcel of files which were edited and passed out to various departments with recommendations for action.

Chapter 21 The Gloves Come Off

The Foreign Secretary was looking forward to this mornings meeting with the Chinese Ambassador. After spending several hours with a grey-suited man and the head of the defence staff the previous afternoon and sitting up till the early hours ploughing through numerous files he would, for once have the upper hand.

"The Chinese Ambassador Minister." announced his secretary.
"Send him in."
The diplomat was shown to a comfortable chair and offered tea or coffee. That was the last time he would be comfortable for the rest of the day.
"I would like you to explain, Mr Ambassador, what is going on inside your Western border?"
" Nothing at all Foreign Secretary. Why do you ask?"
The next hour involved the unfortunate and ill-informed ambassador being brought up to date on what was happening in his home

country by a member of a foreign government. He was then handed a file containing a copy of all the documents he had been shown, told that the Prime Minister expected a call from the Chinese President no later than four o'clock that afternoon then ejected from the Foreign Office with instructions to immediately contact his government.

Within minutes the telephone lines between London and Beijing were red hot.

The small Seeker dragon thrust her head through the portal, blinked to clear the moss and cobwebs which covered the rock wall she was looking from. This was the place. She could feel it in her bones. Seekers had a ring of glands in their necks just behind the flared armoured back of their skulls. These glands were attuned to the magnetic field of whichever dimension they were exploring and acted as a satellite navigation system giving them a precise knowledge of where they were relative to the planets magnetic poles. She was very pleased with the portal she had found. It was shielded by high rock walls and was well above the floor of the mouth of the extinct volcano that contained it. Carefully she climbed from the portal cave and up the rock wall to the lip of the volcano. As she moved the colour of her scales changed to merge with the rock she was climbing. Perching on the weathered edge of the rock she observed the surrounding countryside. This was the place. She could see for miles in every direction despite the poor light and the covering of low, thick cloud which turned the daylight grey. In every direction, she could see scorched fields and the occasional ruined building. What was missing was people. The only sign of life was a small tank followed two trucks heading away to the West.

"Are you going to be sightseeing all day or can I get on enlarging this portal? Is this the right place or not?." The thought came from a rather grumpy Digger dragon who was not best pleased to be sent out with a Seeker who could barely be a century old.

"Sorry, I was just making absolutely sure. I didn't want to waste your time digging in the wrong place. Yes, this is exactly where we should be." She hurried back down the rock wall and squeezed past the Digger went back through the portal and sent her report to the Grand Council along with her estimate of how long it would take the Digger to make the cave large enough for Noble dragons to use.

"Have you found any trace of the missing egg?" asked her contact.

"Nothing at this location but I would only be able to scent an egg within a twenty-mile radius of the portal. Any further would require a flying dragon and Seekers don't fly."

"Thank you little one you have performed the task we set you magnificently. Stay till the Digger has finished then hurry back to join the hunt for the egg."

The Fearsome Four were in Dave's computer centre at the museum helping him to input data from Bird Watch and analyse the results. A large screen on one wall showed a map of the world. Various coloured dots were illuminated in countries across the globe. Red dots showed the location of sites identified as belonging to Quin-T- Sential, while blue dots were the main suppliers to the company. There were more yellow dots than any other colour as these indicated outlets for the company's products. The brighter the dot glowed the more business that site turned over, and just off the coast of China was a pulsing black dot which was the hub of all the activity or the multi-national business.

Ava and Kate were looking at the map.

"You said the Lions said that a warlord had to personally train a War dragon right?" said Kate.

"Yes, why?" asked Ava

"Well, if I was the head of the operation I wouldn't let anyone else go near the egg in case it hatched and imprinted on the wrong individual. "

"So, If that black dot is the headquarters that is where the boss would be and also where the egg would be."

"That's certainly the way I see it." Said Kate.

Ava quickly wrote out a note, rolled it up and prodding Sprocket who was dozing under a bench put it into a small brass cylinder attached to his collar.

"Get this to Llewellyn or Golden Friend as soon as possible." she thought at the small dragon. Sprocket yawned, stretched then hopped onto the windowsill. Victoria opened the window and he jumped out. As soon as he was in the air he ignited his tail jet and with a sonic pop disappeared faster than the speed of sound.

Three pigeons and a seagull had been pecking at the window with reports and Peckerty, Blaggard's wife, hopped forward to translate for the girls while Gil dealt with the first of the pigeons. Pekerty had no problem with the other two pigeons but everyone knew that seagulls were more than a little mad and none of the children could make head or tail of their garbled thoughts so the patient crow teased out the information from its tumbling mind.

As more and more information was added to the database Dave sent it on to the grey-suited man in his small Whitehall office who, in turn, parcelled it out to other departments and fended off any awkward questions about the source of the information.

The President of China, Leader of the Party and Supreme Commander of the largest armed forces on the planet carefully replaced the handset of his telephone, took a deep breath and silently thanked his ancestors that it had not been a video call.

The heads of the armed forces, important Party chiefs and senior government ministers waited for him to explode. They had been silent while the fifteen-minute call had lasted but had only been able to hear what their leader said. He had not said much and most of that had been subdued and placatory despite the colour of his face and neck growing redder by the minute. Fixing his gaze on his military and intelligence chiefs he asked

"How is it that the Prime Minister of Great Britain knows in detail what is happening on our Western border when you find it impossible to offer me a single fact. I have just been put in my place like a naughty schoolboy who has failed to hand in his homework. You!" he fumed pointing at the head of the Airforce."How many aircraft have we lost so far?"

The man shifted uncomfortably, unable to meet his leader's eyes.

"I will tell you that the Prime Minister assures me we have lost twenty-three for the grand total of no information.

Turning to the Minister of the Interior he asked.

"How many check and military bases have we lost and how many troops and police are missing? You have no idea, do you? He shouted before the trembling man could utter a word.

Looking around the cowering group, his expression like a thunder cloud, he lowered his voice to an icy purr.

"You have one hour to get some answers. If at the end of that time you still have none you will be transferred to a labour battalion to serve out the rest of your days. Now get out all of you except you." He pointed at the Head of Intelligence who almost fainted with fear.

"Take this number. Talk to the man who answers. Tell him anything he asks for and get yourself up to speed. It will be your responsibility to co-ordinate with the British and make sure I am not embarrassed again or your life will be forfeited.

Chapter 22   Resistance Begins.

Gil was mooching around the garden. He was bored. The girls were busy inputting data but no birds had reported in for an hour and he had nothing to do. There was a flurry of wings in the tree at the end of the garden and looking up he saw Dodger the crow with a very tattered seagull land in the top branches.

"Hi Dodger, any news?"

The crow flew down and perched on Gil's shoulder.

"That mad gull keeps blathering about hot spots in a rock but I can't make any sense of his thoughts. You know what gulls are like and he won't fly any further. Keeps moaning about the lack of fish."

"Stay here while I get some fish and get your mum to come and talk to it." With that, he rushed off to raid the fridge and fetch the older crow. He found a pair of fresh mackerel wrapped in paper which he took out and laid on the lawn. The gull fell on the fish and began to devour them while Gil rang Victoria and asked her to bring

Peckerty through the portal to interrogate the mad sea bird.

By the time Victoria arrived with Peckerty the gull had eaten both the mackerel, a tin full of sardines and was making hard work of a frozen cod fillet which was thawing in the sun.

There followed a period of squawking, cawing and wing flapping which seemed to go on forever and though Gil could pick out the occasional thought from Peckerty he had no clue what the seagull was thinking. Its mind was a jumbled mass of disjointed flashes and trying to make sense of it was like walking barefoot on a carpet of freshly sharpened hedgehogs.

Peckerty flew up onto Gil's shoulder, while the gull, finding no more fish flapped off in disgust.

"That was awful. Every other thought is 'want fish' or 'need fish'. In the end, I managed to piece together a picture of a fang of rock in a boiling sea with steam coming off it and a white glow deep below the surface somewhere far to the East." Peckerty sighed and ruffled her feathers. "

That was really hard going. I hate talking to seagulls, they're all fish obsessed morons!"

Gill thought back to the large screen with the map of the world on it and the pulsing black dot just off the coast of China.

"Could it have been near China? He asked

"Could be. Geography's not my strong point and it certainly wasn't his." thought the crow. She hopped down to a dish of mealworms while Gil and Victoria headed back to the portal to relay the news to the others.

Having returned from Dragon world, Sprocket was tucking into a hubcap full of barbed wire and rusty nuts and bolts washed down with half a litre of sump oil when Gil and Victoria arrived.

"We may have found the egg." gasped Gil trying to get his breath back.

While her brother explained the information the seagull had brought Victoria brought up the map on the big screen and pointed to the pulsing black dot.

"This place is their H.Q. and is a rock in the middle of the sea as the gull described. We think the egg must be in a room well under the surface because part of the rock is glowing hot and boiling the sea around it. The Seekers need to concentrate on finding a portal into this rock so the Temple Lions can get it back to the female before she does some real damage."

Sprocket lapped up the last drops of engine oil then launched himself out of the window and ignited his tail jets once again.

When he arrived back in Dragon World the meeting place was seething with dragons coming and going.

He relayed the new information to Llewellyn who was organizing the portal search. Golden Friend meanwhile was checking out the team of dragons who were preparing to go through the portal to the volcano.

By the time the children arrived Golden Friend and his team had left and the last of the Seeker and Digger teams were filing into various portals to continue the search for the egg. Llewellyn was left at his lectern to explain to the children what was happening and to bring them up to date with the dragon's progress. He took them across to the library where several small Artisan dragons were busy adding details to a three-dimensional map. It showed all the points of interest that were on the big screen map in Dave's office but on a transparent overlay of Dragon World was marked all the portals the Seekers were exploring and where they linked to in Human World. The main point of interest was the Volcano portal near the Western border of China. This was where Golden Friend and the reconnaissance squadron had made their base. Ever-changing dotted lines showed the track of each dragon as it explored its search area. The other centre of activity was around a group of jagged volcanic spurs of rock sticking out of the sea off the Chinese coast. One particular island was marked in red and at present showed no portals but portals had been found on four islands close by.

"We are concentrating the Seekers on this group of islands and the sea surrounding has been cordoned off from shipping by Marine Serpents who are preventing any boats from coming within a fifty-mile radius of the target island. A combination of our dragons and the Chinese Airforce ar enforcing a No-Fly zone around the same area."

"Won't the people on the island notice what is going on?" asked Victoria.

"They will notice eventually that nothing is coming close to the island but they were keeping most sea and air traffic away themselves. Our dragons don't appear on radar screens and the Sea Serpents are invisible to radar and sonar sweeps, so nothing unusual will show up on their screens. It will be many days before they start to worry." Llewellyn assured the children.

A young female dragon who's name translated as Flame Dancer was patrolling the West China border and skimmed through the wisps of the cloud base. As she glided her head moved from side to side scanning the featureless countryside on either side of the invisible demarcation line. Nothing was happening and nothing had happened for the four hours she had flown back and forth along her patrol area. She began to drop her left wing to circle back for the return journey. Another four hours of this inaction before she could return to the Volcano portal for food and rest. Her head drifted to the right as she began the turn then a bright white spark caught her eye. It was close to the ground near a fold in a line of low hills, but as she watched it grew brighter and began to climb rapidly. Turning more tightly and driving down her wings Flame Dancer gave chase broadcasting an alarm call to the rest of the squadron as she went.

She could see it clearly now as the distance closed. In shape and characteristics, it flew like the little Scrap dragons, propelled by a tail jet its wings folded almost flat to its body. Much larger, almost ten times as long as the small dragons and much more bulky. As far as she could judge its cruising speed was well below that of a Noble dragon like her and much slower than the small dragons who could easily exceed the sound barrier when using their jets.

The direction of flight was inland from the border towards the leading edge of the cold front which was causing all the cloud. Flame Dancer dipped below the cloud base and scanned ahead. Her eyes, developed for hunting the skies allowed her to focus on a column of military trucks over a hundred kilometres ahead and the device was heading directly for it. She could easily see the flame of its jet though her blue-grey colouring and wing driven flight made her nearly invisible. The craft overflew the convoy then banked into a climbing turn and increased its flame to gain height quickly. At the apex of its climb, the device flipped over and plummeted earthward followed by the dragon. Passing through the sound barrier as its speed increased the aircraft, for that was what it appeared to be, swooped towards the convoy with the dragon on its tail. Flame Dancer smelled the inflammable liquid even before it started to be released and knew instantly that it intended to incinerate the convoy. As the first drops of silver liquid fell from the aircraft, the dragon shot fire from her flame ducts. The explosion was thunderous and a huge fireball flowered in the sky just behind the last truck of the convoy. Snapping her wings shut Flame Dancer arrowed through the ravening fire and arced upward, her powerful wings clawing for altitude. Below her, the convoy scattered and as eyes searched the sky for the cause of the attack she disappeared into the gloom of the clouds.

In the control room, a drone pilot stared at his screen which had suddenly gone blank. No warning, no feedback from his drone. One minute the camera feed showed the perfect attack course and fuel release, the next a blank screen. No sheet of fire, no explosion. Nothing.

In the next half hour, four more drones suffered total failure and the officer in charge terminated launches until all drones were overhauled and the fault found.

As the news of the drone kills came back through the Volcano portal cheers and hoots of triumph could be heard from the library. While in his office in Whitehall the man in the grey suit smiled as he replaced his telephone receiver having been told of three convoys and two bases that had witnessed fireballs in the sky above them but had suffered no casualties.

On the jagged rock spur in the sea off the coast of China, the mood was bleak and scapegoats were being sought.

Chapter 23 Cracks Appear

Reports started to come in to the library from the Volcano portal of large groups of people crammed into fenced-off compounds with guards and watchtowers. Sprocket led a party of small Scrap dragons through the portal and in pairs they set out to investigate what these camps were. Landing near one, Sprocket and his companion hid behind some thorn bushes and watched. Before long it became apparent that these were civilians being held captive by armed soldiers. Sprocket spotted one woman who was taller than the rest and whose blond hair stood out from all the other dark-haired prisoners. Asking his companion to keep watch he scampered across the dusty ground and squeezed under the wire fence. Nobody took any notice of what appeared to be a small scruffy dog as it ran past.

Stephanie was attempting to teach basic arithmetic to a group of young children when Sprocket ran up and sat beside her. The children laughed and pointed at him. Stephany tried to ignore him and continued to scratch numbers in the dust with a stick. 2+2 = she wrote. Sprocket hopped forward and wrote 4 with his claw. Stephanie gaped with amazement and the children giggled. She reached out and wrote 25 + 7 =. Sprocket wrote 32. The children clapped. Stephanie tried multiplication and division sums and the small creature answered each one correctly. This went on for some time with the Maths getting longer and more complicated. The children got bored and wandered off to find something more interesting to do while Stephanie continued to try and outwit Sprocket, Finally, Sprocket sat up straight, folded his arms and stared at the woman. Stephanie stared back and became aware of a strange scratching sensation in her mind. Sprocket closed his eyes and really concentrated on pushing his thoughts at the woman.

"Open your mind and listen to me." He repeated the thought again and again till at last Stephanie blinked and said: "Is that you?"

"Don't speak, just think at me then stop and listen with your mind." Came the reply, more clearly this time.

She tried. "What are you and how can you do this?"

"Never mind what I am, I and others of my kind are here to help you and take you to safety. Be ready to get the people moving when I return."

"When will you return and how will we know to start moving?"

"You will know. The signs will be obvious." And with that Sprocket scuttled away and squeezed back under the fence to rejoin his companion.

Back in the Volcano plans were laid. Each pair of Scrap dragons would be accompanied by a Nobel dragon to take care of the guards and by one of the children to calm and lead the human captives away from the camps and back to the Volcano and safety. The Fearsome Four went through the portal and joined the dragon teams, then set off to the first four camps.

Arriving at the camp where Stephanie was captive Sprocket accompanied the Nobel dragon to the hut where the guards slept and ate. Of the twenty guards who manned the compound one shift of ten were having their evening meal. Sprocket set fire to the end of the hut opposite the door and continued to breathe fire till the whole wall was ablaze. The Noble dragon had positioned itself to the right of the hut door and as the panicked guards rushed from the burning building it blew a cloud of bright white fire. This served two purposes. Firstly it illuminated the enormous creature and secondly, it warmed the guards just enough to send them running and screaming away into the darkness as fast as their legs would carry them. The second Scrap dragon was climbing one of the fence posts burning through each strand of barbed wire as it went. Stephanie, seeing what was happening had moved towards the gap in the fence that the scrap dragon was making. She was met by Ava who explained that there was nothing to fear from the dragons and the people should walk out through the gap and gather a safe distance from the burning hut and wait to be guided away. While this was going on Sprocket and the Nobel dragon snapped the legs of the guard towers causing them to topple over, then blowing clouds of white fire to ensure that the guards ran off. Ava climbed onto the back of the Noble dragon and called on the people to follow them to safety. With the aid of Stephanie translating and calming thoughts from the large dragon, the crowd set off towards the Volcano. The two Scrap dragons led the way blowing clouds of bright steam which hung in the air to illuminate the path to follow. Other dragons carrying food parcels and large bottles of water were setting up feeding stations along the way.

Throughout the night camps were liberated and groups of people were led to a tented town by the extinct volcano where they were looked after by aid workers who had been brought in via the portal. As dawn broke a convoy of trucks arrived to begin evacuating the refugees to temporary housing set up by the Chinese government.

A Seeker dragon poked its head through a newly opened portal and rapidly withdrew.
"What's the problem?" asked the Digger dragon accompanying it.

"Lava spout and it's full of molten lava." replied the Seeker "If you dig up fifty metres or so I can sense another portal and I can have a look."

The Digger began to tear at the roof of the passage with its huge claws as the Seeker stepped back. After half an hour of excavation, the Digger dropped out of the shaft it had made.

"Try up there." It said. The Seeker clambered up the shaft. Seconds later the Seeker was back.

"Got it, but we need a Scrap dragon. The portal is well above the lava but the tube needs to be sealed to keep the heat down or when we break through into where the humans are everything will burst into flame."

"I'll go and get one." Said the Digger and bustled back along the tunnel.

On the Western border, Flame Dancer led a wing of four dragons towards the drone launch site. They circled at altitude picking out targets and working out the best plan to put the site out of action permanently. Once they were agreed on the plan of attack they closed their wings and dropped like silent avenging angels. No warning was given and no alarm was raised as four streams of white-hot fire burst across the camouflaged buildings. Metal flowed like water, wood exploded and drums of fuel rose into the air like giant rockets on columns of their blazing contents. Seconds later four dragons disappeared back into the clouds while below all that remained of the drone site was a pool of slowly cooling lava.

Lee Mi emerged from her inspection of the egg. Nothing had changed. Her assistants were extremely careful as they helped her out of the heat resistant armour she needed to enter the hatching room.
"How much longer must I wait for this thing to hatch?" she snapped at the group of trembling historians who were translating the ancient scrolls on dragon taming.
"The scrolls are imprecise on hatching times Ma'am. The instructions are more to do with dealing with the hatchling. How and what to feed it and methods of training. Parts of some of the wording has been burned away."

"Don't give me excuses you drivelling fool. For what you and your team are costing me I expect and demand results."

The historian ducked to avoid the metal covered gauntlet which she hurled at him as she stormed out of the observation room. Things didn't improve when she returned to her office. The pile of reports on her desk were all bad news. Several suppliers had closed down, there had been no contact from five of the internment camps and a report from a truck delivering supplies and spare parts to the drone launch site said that it had disappeared and all that remained was an area of scorched ground with a pool of cooling volcanic glass at its centre.

The rest of the day grew steadily worse as she stormed from department haranguing the hapless staff and still failing to get any clear results.

Chapter 24 Rescue

Stephanie was in shock. In the last few hours, she had been freed from a prison camp by a young girl and myths from the dark ages. She had always prided herself on her down to earth approach to life and the problems it threw at her. Now, dragons turned out to be real. She had been separated from her fellow inmates when the Chinese Army trucks had come to transport them and placed on a small fast helicopter with British markings. In short order, she was flown to a small airfield and transferred to a very plush private jet which whisked her across continents to land at an RAF base in Northern England. During the flight, her wounds had been cleaned and dressed, she had been given six injections to cure or prevent she couldn't remember what and now washed and in clean clothes she was sitting in an office opposite a man in a neat grey suit.

"Thank you for agreeing to this meeting Miss Thompson. Would you prefer tea or coffee? Do help your self to biscuits."

Stephanie breathed out slowly. She was just about keeping a lid on her temper.

"Never mind agreeing. I didn't have much choice in the matter. I have been chivvied from pillar to post for the last day and the last people who showed any real concern for me were a young girl and some huge fire breathing lizards. I would appreciate an explanation. Oh and tea, please."

The man in the grey suit poured her a cup of strong tea and passed it to her whilst pushing forward the tray with milk, lemon slices and sugar.

"Yes. Where to begin? You know part of the story and in truth, we are running hard to catch up. Let me give you some background. During the next half-hour, he laid out the background to the Quin-T-Sential organization, its power-crazed owner and her links to the ancient dragon-riding warlords of the ancient Chinese dynasty. He showed her maps and details of the invasion of the part of China which the Qin had once ruled.

"As you can imagine this whole business is proving immensely embarrassing to the Chinese government. At first, they denied all knowledge of what was going on and it was only when we provided irrefutable evidence of what we knew that they capitulated and co-operated with us to start sorting this business out."

"But what about the news media?" asked Stephanie "The young girl, Ava, is that her name? said that my video had been all over the internet?"

"Ah yes. Your video. Well, Quin-T-Sential did a fair job of discrediting it as a clever stunt and the Chinese government mopped up what they had missed. Everyone knows that dragons don't exist so it had to be a hoax."

"But I've seen them. I've touched them, communicated with them. They were as real as you and me, probably more real than some of the things I've been asked to believe."

"Yes, you and I and a select few other people know dragons are real. But for your own safety and ability to carry on a normal life it would be better to stick with the drone explanation of what happened. Do you really want to spend the rest of your life being regarded as a batty woman who believes that myths exist or would you prefer to keep the secret and meet with others who know the truth such as young Ava, her cousins and their very sensible parents?"

"When you put it like that it seems like the best idea. I remember asking the stewardess on the flight about the dragons and she patted me on the shoulder and suggested I get some sleep. I could see in her eyes she thought I was hallucinating and a bit ga-ga. But I will be able to meet the dragons again won't I?"

"Yes you will, and they want to meet you."

The Digger returned with two Scrap dragons carrying bundles of what appeared to be glass rods. They followed the Seeker up the tunnel to the portal and proceeded to build a platform over the lava tube by weaving the rods into a mesh and fusing them with the smooth sides of the tube. The Digger brought up piles of earth and rock which the Scrap dragons melted and spread to cap the tube. They worked on until the cap became a plug nearly two metres thick, then the Digger enlarged the portal chamber and the lava tube till it was large enough for a

Temple Lion to move through. The team broke through into the headquarters in an all but empty storeroom. Work stopped while the Seeker located the shortest route to the hatchery with its precious egg. Then digging began in earnest. As they broke through into each level the Scrap dragons sealed off any access to their space from the rest of the surrounding rooms and corridors. When all that remained between them and the egg was the hatchery wall the Temple Lion was brought through. He carried with him an insulated cocoon with a Scrap dragon attached to one end to breath fire into the egg chamber and an exhaust tube at the other.

"There is someone in the chamber. We must wait till they leave, then be in and out as fast as possible," thought the Seeker. "As we retreat with the egg I want you to collapse the tunnel behind us and seal it off. There must be no connection left between here and our world."

The rest of the dragons and the Temple Lion nodded and sat down to wait.

The Seeker had just detected the person in the hatchery leaving, when a Scrap dragon who had been looking after the plug in the lava tube and poked his head through the hole in the floor.

"You better get a shift on." he thought " the pressure in the tube is building and the plug could blow at any moment."

The Digger immediately crashed through the wall into the hatchery followed by two Scrap dragons who blackened the crystal window with greasy smoke then set about welding the door shut. The Temple Lion barrelled across to the hearth and with gloved paws lifted the glowing egg onto the cocoon and closed it.

"Breathe fire now and don't stop till we are back in our world," he told the Scrap dragon attached to the front of the cocoon. Steam and flame began to pour from the exhaust tube.

The Digger was gone, already hurrying back along the tunnel towards the portal closely followed by the Scrap dragons and the Seeker. The Temple Lion climbed out of the ruined hatchery and made his way back down the tunnel while the remaining Scrap dragon sealed up the hole. When all the dragons had passed the plug in the lava tube the last one weakened the plug then closed the hole to the portal. Seconds later the plug failed and molten lava rushed up the tube cutting the link to Dragon World with white-hot liquid rock.

Outside the welded door to the hatchery, Lee Mi screamed at the crew to work faster to gain entry to the sealed chamber. Her temper did nothing to speed the operation and when the door and its still attached frame collapsed into the room it was clear their efforts had been in vain. The egg had gone. Only two things stopped her from killing everyone in the room. She had no weapon and the area where the Scrap dragon had closed the hole was now glowing red hot. Everyone ran away except two burly guards who grabbed their screaming boss and carried her kicking and spitting back to her office where they dumped her in her chair then ran for it.

Chapter 25 The Clean Up

There should have been celebrations when the Egg team returned triumphant to Dragon World but there was no time. Pausing to change the Scrap dragon on the cocoon the Temple lion accompanied by six more Scrap dragons headed for the portal back to Ice Fang Mountains. The exhausted Scrapdragons were taken off for a much-needed meal of mixed metal bits with a sump oil and battery acid sauce.

Ken was waiting at the foot of the Temple steps when the exhausted Temple lion arrived and the last Scrap dragon attached to the cocoon had just about run out of fire. Already covered in insulated armour Ken relieved the panting lion of its burden and detached the Scrap dragon then bounded up the steps and entered the hatchery. The group of chanting monks cowering behind protective walls ducked down as he approached the sleeping female dragon on her birthing fire. Carefully, Ken placed the cocoon next to the hearth and unwrapped the egg. He silently lifted it and rolled it into the fire till it rested against the female dragon's side. Then he began to back away. Everything went smoothly until he had almost reached the door when he bumped into a large brass gong on a stand. It wobbled and swung. The frame tilted and the gong went beyond the tipping point. Ken lunged for it and missed and with a clang loud enough to wake the dead it crashed to the floor.

Ken exited the Temple at a dead run followed by a roar and a boiling cloud of fire and smoke. Only by diving headfirst down the steps did he manage to retain any fur on his rear end.

Silence fell and those gathered around the entrance to the Temple gardens held their breath waiting for the appearance of an enraged dragon.

Nothing happened. So they waited. Still, nothing happened. Then there came a long drawn out rattling croak, the sound of a mother dragon purring over her egg. Everyone sighed with relief.

The Chinese government had received a request from London that the area of land near the border be cordoned off for one week while it was checked for toxic substances which they eagerly agreed to. The soldiers patrolling the cordon reported that the only things to be seen were flocks of birds wheeling back and forth above the deserted land. What they couldn't see was that the birds were dropping all sorts of seeds. When night fell dragons took to the sky scattering Scrap dragon pellets all over the area. Nothing happened on the second day until evening when banks of dark clouds began to build. When night fell the soldiers retreated into shelter because it rained. It poured down. It rained in sheets, in stair rods, it rained cats and dogs. To be precise it rained solidly for two days and then the sun came out. A telephone call from the man in the grey suit in London gave the all-clear and the soldiers allowed crowds of civilians back onto their lands. What they found made them gape in wonder. Where there had been baked mud and blackened, dead tree stumps were rice paddies with the crop almost ready for harvest and fully grown shade and fruit trees. The villages which had been reduced to ash and cinder had been replaced with neat rows of huts each containing the basic furniture needed to liv in them. The people were overjoyed. They had expected poverty and starvation, now they were looking at what promised to be the best rice harvest for years.

Off the coast of China, things were far from good. The repair the Scrap dragon had made to the wall of the hatching chamber had only been a temporary patch and after glowing first red, then bright yellow it went white-hot and melted. Boiling liquid rock poured through and started to run out of the door and down the corridors. Long before the patch collapsed panic had set in. People crowded onto the two transport planes in the hangar as the airstrip was run out for takeoff. Others packed every boat and life-raft and paddled rowed and motored away from the rock spur as fast as they could. Airforce jets sent to attack the rock fortress saw the mass evacuation and called up the navy and coast guard to pick up fleeing people.

Inside her office, Lee Mi was incandescent with rage. She screamed commands into the microphone of the public address system but the connection had been cut so no-one took any notice. She threw switches and hammered buttons to lock down the exits but the shutters had been jammed and the doors were thrown off their hinges. She was powerless to stop the rats from leaving her sinking ship. Finally, it dawned on her that she too should escape to live to fight another day. This would not be the end of the mighty Qin dynasty. She pressed the button to call her assistant. When he didn't arrive immediately she stormed through to the outer office. It was empty. Even he had deserted her. Back in her office, she thumbed the button of the lift to take her down to her private jet, Nothing happened. Out through the secretary's office strode Lee Mi her face like thunder. As she came to the general staff lift she hit the button. Nothing, then she noticed that all the floor indicators were alight. She ran to the fire escape stairs and went down them two at a time. Reaching the next floor she went through it like a tornado. Flinging open door after door she found every one empty. Back at the stairwell she started down but became aware of the heat and the smell of burning. Peering over the bannister to the floors below she could see a fiery glow. As she stared the redness bubbled and gobs of thick liquid were flung into the air. For the first time in her life, she felt fear. Quickly she retreated to her office then through to the garden beyond. Even out in the open air it was hot and the sky seemed obscured by mist. She had nowhere else to go. The last four metres of the surrounding rock walls were polished as smooth as glass to reflect in the sunlight. Lee Mi was trapped.

High overhead in a circling fighter jet the pilot and navigator looked down over the left-wing.

"Will you look at that!" exclaimed the pilot, staring at the seething mass of water surrounding the jagged rock spire. For almost half its height it glowed a deep red and steam and fumes rose from it

"I wouldn't want to be down there. Did they get everyone off? It looks about ready to blow." said the navigator.

"You're right, we are out of here." He centred the controls, opened the throttle and headed for the horizon. Behind them, the air was split by a thunderous explosion which hurled rock, ash and fire high into the sky.

"Just in time." muttered the navigator sending a silent prayer to his ancestors.

News of the explosion off the Chinese coast came through to the small office in Whitehall from the head of Military Intelligence in Beijing and the man in the grey suit issued orders for all Quin-T-Sential premises to be raided and shut down. This message went out worldwide and the long arm of the law swept through what remained of the business empire. At the same time, the message came through to Dave's office at the museum in Batherby Bridge and one of the Scrap dragons working on the sorting lines deep in the mine took it through the portal to Dragon World. The dragons and children gave a collective sigh of relief. There would be celebrations, but not yet.

Chapter 26 All Neat and Tidy

Stephanie had received an invitation and a first-class rail ticket. As a result, she boarded the early train to Leeds. She was shown to a seat in the restaurant carriage and told by the waiter that breakfast would be served as soon as the train was underway.

"Would you prefer tea or coffee while you wait, Madam," asked the waiter.

"Tea please." She replied

"And for me as well."

Stephanie looked up to see the man in the grey suit smiling down at her.

"Rather an early start, but it should be quite a day. I'm looking forward to it. They don't let me out often in case I frighten the public." He said taking his seat opposite her.

"Any idea of what to expect?" she asked

"When it involves dragons, who knows."

The tea arrived and the train pulled smoothly out of the station.

In 7A Pudding Founders Lane all was organised chaos. Four children, several dogs and a small dragon all claiming to be starving to death and demanding large amounts of breakfast. Four parents and Brassroyd trying to make sure they didn't get egg, milk or jam all over their smart clothes. And outside five crows tapping at the window for their morning helping of mealworms and mixed scraps. Gradually the pandemonium subsided as mouths were filled with food and conversations waned in favour of eating.

After breakfast, they all trooped off to the pithead yard, with Brassroyd and Mrs Mumbly in the lead and the crows circling overhead. They had just arrived when a taxi pulled in through the gates. It stopped by the office building and Stephanie and the man in the grey suit got out. Ava ran across to greet Stephanie and introduce her to the rest of the gathering and Neil shook hands with the man from Whitehall. Soon Howard arrived with his family and the adults went inside while the children chased around the yard with Sprocket and the dogs. Mrs Mumbly, being now rather long in the tooth for boisterous fun lay by the office wall in a patch of early sunshine chewing on a lump of bone. Finally, a second taxi arrived and the Chinese Ambassador alighted. He fussed around the boot of the car while the driver struggled to get a large wooden box out and onto the floor without doing any damage to himself or the box. Neil came out of the office block, fetched a four-wheeled trolley and helped the perspiring driver to put the box on it. When everyone had been introduced the group filed over to the pithead lift and entered the cage to make the descent to the lowest level of the mine. Leaving the cage at the bottom of the shaft they approached the striped rock face. Brassroyd took Stephanie's hand and with Mrs Mumbly at his side walked steadily towards the rock wall.

"Don't thee worry lass, just keep hold of me and keep walking." he said to her.

As she neared the striped rock it seemed to fade and become less real. When her foot should have hit the stone it passed into it and with the next step she was through and entered a short cave with the sun shining in at the cave mouth. Dog, man and girl stepped out into the bright pink sunshine and onto the cliff path leading down to the red grassed meeting place, where to her joy she could see a crowd of dragons waiting to greet them. The next three through were Ava, her dog Cupcake and the man in the grey suit. There was no hesitation on his part as this was his second trip to Dragon World. The rest of the group passed through the portal leaving only Neil with the Ambassador and the trolley with the large wooden box on it.

"Take hold of my arm and don't let go," Neil told the Ambassador. "Just walk steadily and keep moving. As we get to the rock wall you will see it fade and we will walk through it. No trouble at all."

They began to walk and Neil felt the ambassador's grip tighten on his arm.

"Just relax." murmured Neil and they stepped through the portal.

As they walked from the cave and onto the cliff path the Ambassador gasped and stopped in his tracks staring at all the dragons gathered below on the red grass.

"It's a bit of a shock seeing real dragons for the first time isn't it?" said Neil. They converse mind to mind which is why you can't hear anyone speaking. When you feel the touch of a dragon's mind try to relax and open your mind to their voices. They don't read minds but just send and receive thoughts from the person they are conversing with. Dragons won't smile at people until they really know them because most Humans are terrified by smiles with so many sharp teeth in them. Concentrate on the calm feeling of their thoughts."

They had now reached the bottom of the cliff path and a large red dragon stepped forward and bowed to Neil and the Ambassador.

Welcome to Dragon World Mr Ambassador." The calm tone and feeling of friendship in the greeting soothed his mind and the Ambassador. "My name is Llewellyn, and I am the secretary to the Council of Noble Dragons. Come to the refreshment tables where you can meet the other members of the Council and try some of the delicacies particular to our world." Neil and the Ambassador walked with the red dragon to where the rest of the visitors and dragons were mingling and tasting the many dishes available. Various dragons introduced themselves and quite quickly the Ambassador began to relax and find it easy to converse mind to mind with the dragons.

Stephanie was having a wonderful time. With the aid of Ava and the other children, she had been introduced to most of the Grand Council then taken off to meet many of the other types of dragon such as the Seekers, Diggers, some of the Artisans and one of the Lifters which had taken her and Kate for a short flight to meet some of the Foresters and see some cheese making with the dinosaurs. They had just landed back at the meeting place when a call came out from Golden Friend for everyone to assemble for the presentations. People and dragons began to find their places in a semicircle around Llewellyn's lectern when a series of hoots was heard from the sky. Everyone looked up scanning the clear pink sky to see where the sound was coming from. High above and out of the disk of the red sun came two Lifter dragons with large bundles dangling from their talons. The pair swooped down pulling up at the last moment, their wings spread to slow their speed, and released their bundles. The bundles immediately developed six legs and hit the ground running. It was a pair of

Temple Lions which Ava instantly recognised as Ken and Jes so she ran to greet them.

"Hello, Ava. Are we too late?" panted Ken as he and Jes grabbed one of Ava's hands each and carried her back to the meeting at a trot.

"Just in time." said the girl as the trio joined the semicircle.

"It's those daft Imperials. They can barely remember their own names let alone get things ready for the presentations on time," grumbled Jes sitting down between Kate and Victoria.

At that point, the red dragon banged on his lectern with a wooden mallet and silence fell as everyone paid attention.

There were many presentations. A huge silver and gold medallion with inlaid scarlet enamel lettering for the dragons pledging eternal friendship from the Peoples Republic of China. There were Red Star medals for Neil, Howard, Stephany, the man in the grey suit, Dave and each of the children for their service to the people of China. There was an intricately carved wooden chest inlaid with gems containing many tightly rolled scrolls which were copies of the Imperial history for the Library which was accepted by Grey Scale the ancient librarian dragon. There were medals on gold chains for the team of Seeker, Digger and Scrap dragons which had found and helped rescue the egg, and lastly a long and beautifully embroidered silk banner from the Dragons to the Chinese People who had suffered in the crisis. Many speeches were made countless words spoken and thoughts transferred till finally the official part was over and the fun began. The visitors were given flights to see Dragon World. Ken and Jes gave the children rides galloping towards each other and only sidestepping at the last second to the screams and whoops of joy from their riders. More food and drink was laid out on the tables and consumed as rapidly as the dishes were brought. The man in the grey suit was given a tour of the library by the librarian and spent hours asking and answering questions.

As the sun set, a huge bonfire was lit and much to everyone's surprise, a flight of fifty imperial dragons arrived and put on a breath-taking display of precision flying and aerial pyrotechnics. As darkness fell the humans and dogs made their way up the cliff path to the portal having spent a perfect day on Dragon World.

There was one more surprise for those first-time visitors to another dimension. As they emerged from the lift at the pithead the sun was still shining and they were in plenty of time to catch the afternoon train back to London.

On the other side of the world from Batherby Bridge wavelets lapped on the shore of a small domed island. Nothing grew on the atoll and in places steam rose from fissures in the rock and shale which made up the low mound in its centre. This was all that remained of the lair of the Dragon Empress. In decades to come tales and myths would arise about the Dragon Woman who tried to tame dragons and rule the world but nothing disturbed the atoll.

In a small town in Northern China, a man with no tongue opened a school and taught deaf children and those with no speech in sign language. Many sought his help but his fame didn't spread because he only served children and shunned all publicity. His life was simple and he was content.

List of Characters and Places

The Humans:

Arthur Kitchener Mountbatten Brassroyd: Owner of Brassroyd Environmental

Neil Robert Brassroyd: Son of Frederick Lebassy Windsor Brassroyd and Eleanor (Nelly) Threepstock, both deceased, and nephew of Arthur.

Louise Brassroyd: Neil's wife and Ava's mum. Met Neil when they both worked for The Council

Ava (10): Daughter of Neil and Louise. The fourth member of the Fearsome Four

Jill: Neil's sister, mother of the Cousins, and the aunt that Ava adores.

The Cousins: Victoria (14), Kate (12) and Gilbert (Gil 10): Jill's children and the other three of the Fearsome Four.

Simon: Jill's husband and father of Victoria, Kate, and Gilbert (Gil). Ava knows that he mends people and thinks he is wonderful.

David Bertwhistle: (Nerdy Dave) IT genius and Neil's friend.

Howard: A friend of Neil's from school days. He had always been tall and still towered above all his friends.

Stephanie Thompson: Aid worker and paramedic working with rural peasants on the Western border of China

The man in the grey suit (Puzzels): Specialist in foreign affairs, in particular, China.

Qin Lee Mi: Owner of Quin-T-Sential company and descendant of the Qin Warlords of ancient China. She intends to be the new Dragon Empress.

Chan: Lee Mi's mute secretary and assistant

Temple Monks: Resident in the realm of the Imperial dragons. It is their job to look after the female Imperial dragons while they lay and hatch their eggs.

Animals and Birds:

Mrs Mumbly: An English bull terrier belonging to Brassroyd (though she believes that Brassroyd belongs to her). She found the dragon egg and has brought Sprocket up like her own pup. Now she has five proper pups of her own.

Blaggard: A crow who lives with his family in the birdhouse in the garden of number 7 and 7A Pudding Founders Lane. He thinks he is occult but he's not. All crows think they are occult.

Peckerty, Faithless, Shiftless and Dodger: Blaggard's family.

Places:

Batherby Bridge: Centre of the Five Fells District and once again, a thriving market town with an expanding craft industry.

The Dragons:

Sprocket: A lesser Scrap Dragon hatched from an egg in the kitchen at 7 Pudding Founders Lane. Scrap Dragons come in two sizes, Lesser and Greater, though the Greater is only about a metre and a half long from nose to tail

Golden Friend: A large golden coloured Noble Dragon who visits Neil and shows him the Dragon World.

Llewellyn Ap Griffith: A large red Welsh Noble Dragon who is secretary to The Grand Council of Noble dragons

Grey Scale: Possibly the oldest dragon on Dragon World and Keeper of the Library of all Dragon Knowledge.

Flame Dancer: Young female Nobel dragon. Finder of the drone launch site - she leads the attack which destroys it.

Seekers: Path-finder dragons who search out new portals within and between worlds. They are black in colour and have long snouts and necks. Their heads and necks are heavily armoured with larger, thicker scales in case when they poke their heads through a new portal there is something nasty on the other side. Though normally black, they can change the colour of their scales to blend with their background, and so disappear.

Lifters: Medium-Sized dragons, brown in colour, with very large, rectangular wings which can lift heavy weights and pull large loads. Their hind legs are quite short but very powerful and their feet have six toes, four at the front and two at the back to give extra grip.

Diggers: Tunneler dragons with large shovel-shaped front feet, each equipped with ten, diamond-hard claws. Their hind feet have hard side fans for pushing spoil back behind them and they have ridges in their belly scales which act as a conveyer belt to move soil and rock fragments down to the back feet.

Artisans: These are the dragons who make all the tools and gadgets which the other dragons and creatures need and use. They are also expert in dragon medicine and collect, store and dry thee many herbs and plants dragons need to keep fit and well.

Imperial Dragons: Descendants of the dragons of ancient China. Consider themselves to be superior to all other lifeforms. In fact, they have not evolved in centuries and because they are short-tempered live cut off from the rest of Dragon World by the ocean on one side and the surrounding Ice Fang mountains which surround them.

Temple Lions: Fire breathing but flightless dragons. Six legs but no wings. They can stand and walk on their four back legs. The front pair double as arms and hands.

Ken and Jes: Two Temple Lions that Ava meets. Like others, they guard the Temples which are the hatcheries for the Eggs of Imperial dragons

Time Difference: 1 year in Dragon World = 30.5 days in Human World.

Contact details:

email: penworkspublishing@gmail.com

If you have any questions, find me on Facebook and post them on my page or send me an email. I will do my best to answer them and if I don't know the answers I will ask Mr Brassroyd if I can have a look at some of his many old and dusty books about Dragons and if that fails I will ask Sprocket.

If your questions are about dogs or crows I will ask Sprocket as he can talk to Mrs Mumbly and Blaggard, unfortunately, I can't.

You can visit my website at:

http://bryanpentelow.wix.com/bryan-pentelow

Best Regards

Bryan Pentelow (Dragon Friend)

Printed in Poland
by Amazon Fulfillment
Poland Sp. z o.o., Wrocław